I0598822

The Descendants

THE WOLVES AND THEIR CIPHER

K.E. TURNER

ENTWINED PUBLISHING

The Wolves and Their Cipher
ISBN # 978-1-80250-619-8
©Copyright K.E. Turner 2025
Cover Art by Kelly Martin ©Copyright December 2025
Interior text design by Entwined Publishing
Published by Eternal, an Entwined Publishing imprint

Published in 2025 by Entwined Publishing, United Kingdom.

Entwined Publishing is a division of Totally Entwined Group Limited.

THE WOLVES AND THEIR CIPHER

Dedication

For all the identical twins out there, who have an incredible bond, but who want to be seen for who they are — individuals. The people who care about you always do.

Acknowledgements

Like all my books, they wouldn't be the same without the support and assistance of numerous people. I'm extremely lucky to have two fabulous beta readers, Danni Line and Victoria Brown, who never fail to be honest with me when they read my manuscripts, even when they know I might not want to hear what they have to say. They are worth their weight in gold.

To my editor, Rebecca Scott, who must want to tear her hair out every time I capitalize things I shouldn't and don't when I should. I'll do better in my next manuscript. Hopefully. To my cover designer Kelly Martin, thank you for bringing to life my characters. To Angela Brannon for reading over some of the more technical aspects of this book and making sure I didn't make a fool of myself with inaccuracies. I'm so grateful for your help. To my family who support me, no matter how spicy my books get—it means everything to me. And to my wonderful readers who've followed from my original series, and those who've found me through this one, you're the best.

Author's Note

Dear Reader,

When I encounter foreign words I do not know the meaning of in a book, it causes me to pause each time I see them in the text, taking me out of the story. Here is a brief list of foreign words and meanings I have used in this book.

Alor: So
Bébé: Baby (Term of endearment)
Bonbon: Slang for clit
Café: Coffee
Chérie: Sweetheart, dear
Connard: Asshole
D'accord: Okay
Fille: Girl
Fils de pute: Son of a bitch
J'ai veux la mordre. De la revendiquer: I want to bite her. Claim her.
Merde: Shit
Minou: Pussy
Mon amour: Love, or my love
Non: No
Oui: Yes
Pirate Informatique: Information Pirate – hacker
Putain: Fuck
Salut: Hi
Soutien-gorge: bra
Terrior: a French term used to describe the environmental factors that affect a crop's phenotype, including unique environment contexts, farming practices and a crop's specific growth habitat.
Tête de noeud: Dickhead

Prologue

Paris
March

Pierre ripped his headset off, flung it on his keyboard and scrubbed his face with his hands. "*Putain.*" He leaned back in his chair and stared at his screens, his latest deep-dive into asset records drawing a blank. Again. "If it weren't so frustrating, I think I'd have a hard-on for this hacker. Whoever it is, they're good."

He checked the time. Eight a.m. Another all-nighter. Damn, he was tired. He glanced at the blackout blinds, tempted to roll them open. When was the last time he'd stepped outside? He wouldn't even know it was spring if not for the date at the bottom of his screen.

Maxime, their pack's alpha, had been riding them for weeks. They needed to find this woman. Too much was at stake. Cordelia King was a thorn in everyone's side. Who knew what the witch was planning. His brother Gabriel had called him again yesterday, concerned about the unrest in the coven his new mate Annabelle governed. And Isobella, his soon-to be-great ancestor, was prepped and ready for her journey back in time. They couldn't hold off any longer. Isobella's health was deteriorating.

"Here." Louis handed him a Red Bull. "I think we can agree there's more than one hacker. And they're not working as a team, either. She's hired them individually."

He cracked the can and took a swig, the pop and fizz of liquid adrenaline a welcome boost to his fatigued mind. His trash can was full of empties. They'd been living on the stuff of late. When they'd started this quest, they'd been full of confidence, certain they'd have her by New Years. How hard could it be to find one little old lady?

"*Oui*. Unless she's racking up more frequent flyer points than half the corporate world, she's got hackers in a dozen countries." He ticked off his fingers. "The US, the UK, Australia, China, Switzerland, Russia. Hell, I cracked one of her identities in Uzbekistan yesterday."

"I doubt she'd be in Uzbekistan."

"Agreed."

Louis flopped into his chair, spinning it so he faced Pierre and not his own set of screens. "I've been thinking. Maybe we're going about this all wrong."

"Mmm?" He'd give his left testicle for a fresh idea, a different angle, anything to get them the result they needed.

"We've been chasing our tail for three months now." Louis opened his can of Red Bull. "How many times have we been through this since Christmas?"

Every time they'd get a hit with the facial recognition software they'd hijacked, they'd track her digital trail to a dead end. Another fake identity. Then she'd pop up again in another city, another country.

"Too damn many to count. But what's the alternative? Boots on the ground aren't going to help unless we have somewhere to send them."

"Maybe" — Louis swiveled back to his screens, setting his drink aside — "we're going after the wrong person." He tapped on his keyboard and brought up an elegant piece of malware they'd worked on together.

Pierre scooted his chair across the floor until they were side by side. "You mean go after one of the hackers?"

Louis shrugged. "They'd have to have some contact with her — instructions, bank account details. This sort of work doesn't come cheap."

"Which hacker do we target?"

Louis pulled up a screen with a British passport for a June Halliday, a date and place of birth — all fake — Cordelia's wrinkled face and her two different colored eyes staring at him. June Halliday — the real June Halliday — had died in 2022.

"The hacker who created this one has IDS alerts set up. We set off the alarm, insert our malware and hope our code gets us into their systems before we're shut out."

It was a bold move, using the intrusion detection system alerts to hack the hacker. Could they pull it off? "This won't be some geeky kid with computer skills. This is a hacker for hire. They'll be protecting their own identity as much as Cordelia's."

"Well, I, for one, don't want to spend another three months chasing after more of Cordelia's fake identities. Do you?" Louis crossed his arms. "There's two of us against one. And we're good. Even if the IDS alerts have a kill switch — "

"They will."

" —there should still be a small path for admins. We'll get *something*. Maybe not enough to find Cordelia, but enough to give us a lead on the hacker." Louis smiled, vicious canines extending. "Then we pinpoint their location and pay them a visit."

Pierre liked the sound of that. Too many hours spent with no results was pissing him off. Some payback was in order.

He raised his hand in a fist. His twin did the same, and they bumped knuckles. "Let's do it."

Pierre pushed back to his own side of the room, energized for the first time in weeks.

Chapter One

London
April

Melinda Cheng stepped off the Tube at Baker Street station and resisted the urge to quicken her steps. With her laptop bag slung over her shoulder, she kept her pace measured and calm, the prickle on her neck not diminishing as she made her way up to the street. She was being paranoid. It was a coincidence. The events of the last three months had her on edge, seeing things that weren't there. Or maybe not. She'd learned to trust her instincts a long time ago, and they'd never let her down.

The familiar façade of her building loomed, but Melinda kept walking. The last thing she wanted, if she were being followed, was to reveal where she lived. If she hadn't already.

At a boutique clothing store, with its display of the latest spring fashions, she stopped and stared at the large window. That she wouldn't be caught dead in any of this year's newest fashions was irrelevant. She ignored the clothing, focusing on the reflection of the street. Clichéd, but effective. Shoppers strolled or rushed past. A half-full open-topped tourist bus momentarily blocked her view of the opposite side of the street, but he wasn't there. He hadn't followed her off the train?

She ambled past a few more shop windows and stopped again. Nope. Still couldn't see him. Maybe she *had* been imagining things. But… London was home to millions of people. What were the chances of running into the same man three times in one day?

She casually spun around, as though trying to decide which shop might interest her. Still no sign of him. If he hadn't looked like he'd stepped off the pages of some magazine, or a billboard advertisement for Calvin Klein, she might not have noticed him. No. She would've noticed him. There was a sense of danger about him that couldn't be ignored, no matter how handsome he was. She would've picked him out of a crowd of one hundred thousand or more. Her radar to dangerous men had been tuned since childhood.

As though on impulse, Melinda stepped into a bakery. With a quick glance at the patrons to make sure *he* wasn't one, she placed an order to go and waited by the counter, keeping a close eye on the people walking past. With how she earned her money, there was always a risk. Some of her clients weren't the altruistic kind.

But she was certain this was about one in particular. One who had more in common with the women she helped than those she used for income. Username — MysticMage. Based on the photo sent to Melinda, she was an octogenarian. On the dark web. That was a first.

For her, at least. Most of the clients she helped were much younger.

MysticMage hadn't *said* it was a husband she was running from, but Melinda had recognized the signs. She'd read between the lines. Four times she'd created a new identity for her, only to have someone crack it wide open. For goodness' sake, the woman was in her eighties. Couldn't her husband let her live out the last few years of her life in peace? Obviously not, because when they'd hacked Melinda's fifth attempt at creating her a new identity, the hacker had done something else. He'd sent malware through her IDS alerts.

She'd been out of her chair, ripping out the router cable and shutting the computer down within seconds. Her kill switch would have activated, but if the hacker was good—and the past few months told her he was— he would try for the SSH, her network communication protocol. Pulling the plug was the only way to completely cut off access. Had she been fast enough? Had he got enough information to track her location? For there could be no other reason for the malware. She'd been jittery ever since.

Maybe she should take a holiday. Tell MysticMage she'd need to find another hacker and go somewhere warm and sunny, with white beaches and blue water. Where no one would think to look for her. Somewhere like the Greek Islands. She'd always wanted to go.

No. She'd promised she'd keep her client safe, and she was going to damn well do her job. She'd need to take extra precautions, that's all. And back trace that malware without giving up more than she already had. Then she'd send him a nasty little virus of her own for his trouble.

She accepted her tea, turned to leave, and froze. At the counter was *the* guy. There was no mistaking him.

Black Henley stretched across a broad chest, snug jeans hugging muscular thighs, the bronzed skin, the dark hair curling at his nape. Like a Spanish sex god. Or a celebrity. As he perused the cake display, the young female server grinned at Melinda and winked, mistaking her open-mouthed stare for interest.

She snapped out of her trance and waggled her eyebrows at the server, giving the Spanish sex god the once over. Not because she was admiring the taut, rounded globes of his ass, but because she was looking for something that might give her a hint to his identity. A gang tattoo, or…or a leather cuff about his wrist with the silver motif of a… Was that a wolf or a dog?

Okay, maybe she lingered a little on his ass. Before he noticed her staring, she smiled again at the server and walked past the Spanish hottie as though he were nothing more than a momentary distraction.

She dumped her tea in the trash and hurried across the street to a bookstore, browsing the recent releases, her attention fixed not on any book, but on the bakery entrance. The guy with the perfect ass exited, coffee and a paper bag in hand, and turned down the street away from her building. *Huh.* Maybe she was being overly suspicious of him. Seeing him four times in one day *could* be a coincidence. If he lived in the neighborhood. She'd never seen him before, though. She shook her head. This business with the malware had her spooked.

After a few more turns down the street and no further sighting of the hottie, Melinda entered her building. In the empty lift, she leaned against the back wall, letting the tension ease from her shoulders. It'd been a tough day all round. She had a mind to whip up some comfort food — a quick stir-fried egg with tomato. *Mm, yeah.* Her stomach rumbled.

The door was almost closed when a hand and wrist, with a leather cuff and silver motif, shoved between them and the door bounced back open. Melinda stiffened.

Get the hell outta here.

Six-foot something of black Henley and snug jeans smiled perfect white teeth at her. "Thought I was going to miss it."

A thick accent... Not Spanish, though she could have sworn he had at least some Spanish or Latino heritage. French, maybe? He glanced at his watch as he and a waft of spicy aftershave joined her in the lift. She resisted the temptation to breathe him in. A man who was potentially stalking her shouldn't smell that good.

Melinda smiled back, her hand tightening around the strap of her bag. She adjusted her glasses, partially hiding her face as her gaze skimmed over him. Had his hair been a smidge longer? The shadow of a stubble on his chin darker? Numbers glowed from the control panel, but it was the watch on his wrist when he leaned over to punch the button to close the doors that held her attention. A platinum Roger Dubuis Excalibur. She hadn't noticed *that* in the bakery. Strange.

The doors slid shut before she could will her feet to move.

"What floor?" he asked.

He raked a hand through his hair. The action, the stretching of his shirt, the tautening of biceps... *Is it hot in here?* She wanted to fan her super-heated face. Her attention snagged again on that watch.

She cleared her throat. "Um, eight," she lied. "Thank you."

His eyebrows pinched together. "Are you sure?" His hand hovered over the control panel.

She lifted her chin. "Yes. Sorry, long day."

With a shrug, he punched floor eight and floor nine. *Nine.* Her real floor.

He leaned against the elevator wall, hazel eyes framed by long lashes no man deserved to be born with, giving her the once over. Bedroom eyes. Cute. Smoldering. An image of him, naked, tangled in her sheets, rose unbidden.

What the hell, Melinda?

They stood in silence, Melinda staring at the numbers lighting up as the lift rose, the weight of his stare burning holes in the side of her face.

Why is the lift so damn slow today?

She risked another peek. The man could be a bodyguard, with all that muscle. Or a bouncer. Or an underwear model. He'd look good in nothing but a pair of boxer briefs. That bronze skin, the dark shadow on his jaw. Would he have a happy trail?

Or... He could be a private investigator, or a thug sent to intimidate the location of her client out of her.

Or not. Those jeans were snug, and there was no evidence he was concealing a weapon. Her gaze dipped to his crotch. She doubted he'd be hiding a gun there. At least, not the type of gun she was imagin— She cut the thought off, sucking in a deep breath of aftershave.

He pushed himself off the wall, and her gaze followed the flex of muscles across his abdomen up his chest and... *Oops. Busted.* Heat crept up her neck, and she turned away, but not before she caught the flare of his nostrils, and... Was that a...*growl*?

The lift dinged, lurched to a halt, and the door slid open. Melinda dipped her head at him, escaped the confined space and strode down the corridor as if she did, truly, live on this floor. As soon as the lift doors slid shut, she raced for the stairs. Above her, a door closed, then she was alone in the cool stairwell.

With her laptop on the top step and the click of a few commands, Melinda logged into her secure wireless router and pulled up the security feed from the ninth floor.

There he is.

Without a glance at her door, he continued down the corridor to one at the end. *Huh.* Old Mrs. Bellamy had moved out last week. Her kids must have finally put her into that care home they'd been pushing for. He *wasn't* following her? He was her new *neighbor?*

On the grainy security feed, he shifted his coffee and his pastry bag to one hand and retrieved his key.

Wait. What?

Melinda froze the image. He held a takeaway coffee cup and a pastry bag. And there, as obvious as the bulge in his pants had been, was a naked wrist. This *wasn't* the guy in the lift. He wasn't wearing an Excalibur watch.

What the hell?

She tapped a few keys and unfroze the image. Mr. No-Watch was gone — the door to Mrs. Bellamy's flat closed — but striding down the hall *was* the guy from the lift. Mr. Excalibur. She heaved out a sigh. Twins. Her new neighbors, they were twins. But the question remained — what was a man doing living in this building when he could afford to spend two hundred and fifty thousand pounds on a *watch*?

Chapter Two

Pierre leaned against their apartment door and closed his eyes, the enticing scent of their target hacker clinging to his nostrils. A deep rumble threatened in his chest and his cock pressed against the zipper of his jeans. She was a tiny little thing, barely reaching his shoulder, but there was a fierceness about her, a boldness in her gaze, and a stubborn tilt to her chin that had nearly had him pushing her up against the wall and fucking her in the damn elevator.

Putain. That was more Louis' style than his. He shook his head, tamped down on his wayward dick and strode down the hall to where Louis was munching away on his latest foray into British *gâteaux.*

Louis licked his lips and held out the sticky confection. "Chelsea bun. Want some?"

He screwed up his nose. His brother was determined to work his way through every unique variation of what passed for pastry here in London. It was lucky he was a shifter or his penchant for all things food, especially of the sweet variety, would see him wider than the *Place de la Concorde.*

His twin shrugged. "*D'accord.* More for me. Your *café* is on the table."

Louis flopped on the hideous floral couch. Convincing the previous tenant to sell up, furniture and all, had been a boon — as long as they were willing to put up with nineteen-forties old-lady décor. Pierre needed a decent *café* to face it each morning. Thankfully, the *pâtisserie* down the street catered to both his and Louis' needs.

Pierre sucked down a fortifying gulp of caffeine and joined his brother on the couch. "You ran into her in the *pâtisserie*?"

"*Oui*, and while I'd love to say she was admiring my ass while I was making my selection, I'm more confident she was sizing me up as a threat."

Pierre had had the same thought in the elevator. Although, there had been *some* interest. His cock perked up. "She's a hacker. She's bound to be wary. And she did detect our malware."

Louis smirked. "Not quick enough. Not before we got what we needed."

"What else do we know about our little Black Hat, Melinda Cheng?"

"Mm, not so much a Black Hat as a White Hat. Maybe. I did a little research on that building you said she went into." Louis flipped open his laptop and pulled up an image of the nondescript block of apartments she'd visited this morning. "Turns out it's a women's refuge. Not as well hidden as they would like to believe. It's government funded."

"What's she doing at a women's refuge?"

"I did some digging while I was waiting for the Tube. I couldn't find anything current on our cipher except a name, and I was lucky to get that. No surprises there. But I did find these." He clicked on a tab and brought up a list of recordings. "Historical emergency calls." He clicked on one, and the calm voice of the operator and a trembling voice of a child echoed through the speakers.

"Nine-nine-nine, what's your emergency?"

"Please come quick. He's hurting her again."

"Who, sweetie? Tell me what's happening."

"It's Daddy. He's hurting Mommy again. Dinner was too cold and it made him angry."

"I'm sending someone straight away, sweetheart. You stay on the line with me. Are you safe?"

"I'm hiding in the cupboard. He never finds me here."

There were distant sounds of yelling, a crash, a woman's scream and the line went dead.

"There are more. A lot more. All similar. There are records in the UK police database of officers attending the home of a Jiehong and Huiyeng Lee, multiple times. They offered to press charges, but each time Huiyeng claimed she'd" — Louis tapped the keyboard and brought up one statement after another — "fallen down the stairs, tripped and hit a door, wasn't watching where she was going. The list goes on. On record is their daughter, Mei Lin, as a regular nine-nine-nine caller."

"Mei Lin Lee."

"She goes by Melinda Cheng now." Louis clicked on another tab, revealing a black-and-white photo of a woman in her forties. She wasn't smiling, and her face had the resigned look of someone who'd accepted her fate.

"Is that from an obituary?"

"Oui. This is Huiyeng Lee. She died of a stroke at forty-three. Constant beatings from her husband probably helped that along."

Pierre studied the photo. "Melinda has her eyes, and her chin." He took a sip of his *café* and stared at the sad eyes of Melinda's mother. "So, she couldn't help her mother, no matter how many times she called the police, so now she makes it her mission in life to create fake identities for other battered women? Giving them a chance to escape the life her mother never managed to free herself from?" He frowned. "If that's the case, where does Cordelia King fit into this? The only thing she's running from is us. And she deserves to be running."

"I don't imagine women from a government-funded refuge would pay well. We've been watching Melinda for three weeks, and there's no evidence she does anything but hacking." Louis pointed to the women's refuge on the screen. "My guess? These are her passion projects. Something she does because she wants to. Because she's called to do it. Cordelia could be how Melinda makes her money. Taking on other clients."

Pierre stared at the long list of calls to nine-nine-nine. It was telling she'd chosen her mother's maiden name. She could have given herself any name and disappeared completely into the ether. She could've hacked into the police data system, as Louis had — she was good enough to do it — and removed all the evidence of her childhood, but she hadn't. No. She'd deliberately chosen to leave it there. Like an act of defiance against the man who'd tormented her mother. Melinda Cheng was a crusader.

Pierre rose and paced the floor, his hands fisted at his side, his claws threatening to punch through into his palms. That Cordelia would hire hackers to elude them wasn't unexpected, but of all the ones she could have chosen, that she'd picked one with heart, a White

Hat, to do her dirty work, made him want to rend and destroy.

"Pierre?"

"Mm?"

"You were growling."

"I was?" He was? *What has got into me today?* He was on edge, his whole body prepped for a fight and his wolf hovering close to the surface. He scrubbed his chin. "This would be so much easier if our hacker were some pimply little male."

Louis closed his laptop, and swiveled to face him. "How so?"

"We could break into his apartment, tie him to a chair and beat the answers out of him. Or, at the very least, keep him quiet while we crack the encryption on his tech."

Louis eyed him. "I'm not sure why that isn't still an option."

Pierre rubbed at his chest. It was what they'd planned. Why did he suddenly feel so uncomfortable about it? Because she was a woman?

Louis shrugged. "*Alor*, we wait until she goes to the refuge again and break into her apartment while she's gone."

"Her security on her tech will be almost as good as ours. We'd need days."

Louis shrugged. "Then we take her tech. We'd have all the time in the world then."

"Think, Louis. We do that, she contacts Cordelia, and the witch cuts off all ties and disappears. Any information we glean will be useless. We'd be back at the beginning again, hunting down another of her hackers, at the ass-end of the world in Australia or Russia. I don't speak Russian, do you?"

Louis unfurled himself from the sofa. "*D'accord.* Then we go on the charm offensive. Seduce her. Convince her to tell us all of her secrets."

Putain. His cock liked that idea.

"We are new to the building. We do the neighborly thing and invite her over for drinks and *apéritifs.*"

"What makes you think she'd come, Louis? Everything we've learned about her over the last few days suggests she lives most of her life online."

"Mm, but she's suspicious of us, no? This would be her chance to scope *us* out. If we invite the other tenants on this floor, and a few from the one above and below, she'll think it's safe enough to step inside the lion's den. Or" — he grinned, his canines peeking through — "the wolf's den."

Pierre stared at his brother. That might actually work. "We need to do this soon. We've wasted enough time trying to track Cordelia down."

"I can pick up a few bottles of wine, beer, maybe some rum to make a few mojitos tomorrow. Let's make it Saturday night. We don't want to give her too much time to think about it."

Pierre headed for the door. "I'll go invite our neighbors."

Louis' hand on his shoulder stopped him. "You invite the other neighbors. I'll invite her. You had her all to yourself in the elevator. I barely got a good look at her in the *pâtisserie.*"

Pierre studied his twin. There was a determined set to Louis' shoulders he rarely saw, and dark shadows flitted in his eyes, signaling his wolf was close to the surface. She was affecting him, too.

Could it be…? Could she be…? Fate had a funny way of interfering when it came to the mates of Langeais wolves. It'd happened in the past with their ancestors.

They'd seen it with Laurent and Nathalie. And again with Gabriel when he'd been reunited with his mate Annabelle.

"*Oui.* You should go."

If Louis reacted as strongly to her as he had... It wouldn't be the first time in the history of the Langeais wolves twins had shared a mate.

Chapter Three

Melinda let herself into her flat, keeping a wary eye on the closed door down the hall. She disabled the internal alarm and leaned against the door, the adrenaline rush subsiding, but her body still buzzing. Her new neighbors were *hot*.

A rub of fur wound its way through her legs, and she picked up the little ginger cat and snuggled him against her face. "Have you been a good boy, Manchu? Watching over my flat while I was out?"

Manchu bunted his head against her chin, purring his little heart out. She removed her shoes, reset the alarm, then carried her preferred male company into the kitchen and set him up with a dish of cat food. While he tucked into it with feline gusto, Melinda set the electric kettle to boil. She needed to calm down. Jumping to conclusions wasn't the wisest thing to do. Tea. She needed tea.

From the cupboard, she took out her teapot. She rubbed her hands over it, the clay cool against her palms. It'd been her mother's, and was the only thing she'd kept from her past. Etched into her memory, her mother's gentle smile as she'd poured tea for them both. A shared moment of quiet in their turbulent lives. The ritual, the steeping — it never failed to calm her — as though the act of making tea, the familiar scent and the turning of the teapot wiped away the bad memories, the grief and the anger. If only for a brief minute or two.

Melinda poured boiling water into her pot and swished it around, heating the clay. She repeated the process with her cup, then discarded the water. From the tin of jasmine tea, her mother's favorite, she scooped in the fragrant leaves and covered them in boiling water. Twice she rotated the pot, aiding the infusion, before pouring more boiling water into it and letting the leaves steep.

Calmer, with her cup of tea in hand and the scent of jasmine in the air, Melinda unlocked the second bedroom, punched in her alarm code, switched on the light and plopped into the chair in front of her screens. Sipping at her tea, she brought up her surveillance — the kitchen, the living room, the hall, the front door. She found only Manchu — stretching on the couch, shifting to the windowsill to watch the traffic below, wandering into the kitchen to check his empty food bowl. No one had got past her security and into her flat.

She ran a scan and waited for it to confirm all was clear in her cyber world. It took a lot of expertise to get through her firewalls and security measures, but... She eyed the silent monitor on the left, no longer connected to a router. Whoever was after her client was good. Or had hired someone who was good.

The scan came back clear. She relaxed in her chair.

With a tap of a few keys, she hooked into the building security again, specifically the camera in the corridor outside her and her new neighbors' front door.

All clear. She paused, her fingers hovering over the keyboard. Should she…?

She typed in a few more commands, brought up the building's stored footage files, and clicked on today's, fast-forwarding until she spotted herself leaving. A minute or so later, the door down the hall opened and her new neighbor stepped into the corridor, waiting for the lift to return. On one wrist, the leather cuff. On the other, that expensive watch.

The time stamp clicked down, and the second twin stepped into the corridor with the same leather cuff, but his left wrist was bare. He headed straight for the stairwell. Perhaps Mr. No-Watch liked his pastries a little too much and used the stairs to burn off the extra calories.

She skipped ahead to her return. There. One after the other, they strode down the corridor. Again, no concern for the cameras watching. Like any regular person. Or someone who was deliberately ignoring them, *pretending* to be unaware of their presence.

Had they followed her or not? The timing of their departure and return could be a coincidence. She occasionally ran into Joe from apartment thirty-three. He worked a nine-to-five job in an office, took the metropolitan line to work. On one of the infrequent times she'd had to catch the Tube that early, they'd shared the same car.

Mr. Patel, across the hall from the hottie twins, rarely left his flat, but his son would stop by with his wife and two kids on the weekend. She'd shared the lift with them a few times, spotted them having lunch in the café down the street a time or two.

It wasn't *unreasonable* to expect to run into her neighbors, other people from different floors in her building, too, in the local area. But that watch, the expensive platinum Roger Dubius Excalibur, bothered her. This apartment block wasn't in a shady area of London, but it wasn't somewhere someone who could afford to spend *that* amount of money on a *watch* would live. And the timing? So soon after the malware attack?

Melinda clicked out of the file and into another one, the one from last week. She skipped through the footage, watching their comings and goings. Back another week, then another until she found what she was looking for. On a Monday, three weeks ago, according to the time stamp, she'd left the building at eight. She'd had an appointment with a client at the women's refuge. At eight forty-six, the twins stepped out of the lift carrying overnight carryalls and laptop bags slung over their shoulders.

She back-tracked through the footage, searching for them earlier. No. That Monday was the day they'd moved in. She flicked through the footage again in case she'd missed something — removalists, them arriving with boxes, bags, anything. Even if they'd bought the apartment fully furnished, they'd have personal items — clothes, books, stuff. Nothing.

She returned to the Monday footage, flopped back in her chair and stared at the frozen image on the screen. Two men, both in snug jeans and shirt. All they'd brought with them was an overnight carryall and a laptop bag each.

It reminded her of the day *she'd* moved in. Her laptop bag slung over her shoulder, she'd carried all her worldly possessions in an old shopping bag. Not much — a practical change of clothes, toiletries, her mother's teapot, a few photos. She'd wanted nothing else from her haunted childhood. The memories were baggage enough. Melinda had arrived with little more than they had because she'd made a deliberate choice to leave everything else behind. What was their excuse?

She scanned for Wi-Fi networks, ignoring the familiar ones of her neighbors. Nothing new popped up on the list. A hidden SSID? To the uninitiated, disabling the broadcasting function on your SSID made it secure. It wasn't. Not against someone like Melinda. She initiated a program, let it run its scan and picked up two, but they were ones she already knew about. It could be they hadn't set things up yet, or used public networks. It could be something more sinister.

After ensuring her own system was secure, she brought up the newest identity she'd created for her client. None of her alerts had triggered this time. Everything looked as it should. Finally, an identity that was holding. MysticMage had warned Melinda the person she was hiding from would stop at nothing. That money was no object. It used to surprise her what money could buy—private investigators, police officials, silence. Not anymore.

A knock on her front door interrupted her, and Melinda checked her security feed.

What the hell?

Standing at her door, his fist raised to knock again, was Mr. No-Watch.

Louis stood outside Melinda Cheng's door. He'd already pounded on Mr. Patel's—the old man was nearly deaf—and invited him for their little party. And Joe, the advertising rep in apartment thirty-three. If Melinda were watching, or checked the security feed—which no doubt she would—hers wouldn't be the only neighbor's door he'd knocked on. Nor the first.

The wait was interminable, and he fought the need to fidget. He knocked again. Finally, he picked up the soft footfalls of her tiptoeing toward the door. Humans were always so loud, even when they were trying not to be.

The soft scratch of metal on wood signaled the peephole cover sliding across. He lifted his head, letting her get a good look at him. She'd most likely recognize him as the man she'd met in the elevator. To other werewolves, there was a world of difference between him and Pierre, but humans rarely noticed. If she was observant, she might recollect him being in the *pâtisserie* down the street.

Her scent wafted to him, and he breathed it in. The subtle hint of deodorant, something soft, and peaches—her body wash? Shampoo?—and a healthy dose of wariness. Smart *fille*.

Putain, he wanted her to answer. To open the door so he could look his fill, take in every little nuance, her every micro-expression, not the brief side glance he'd received in the *pâtisserie*. He needed more. A few minutes at least. Just him and her. Something about her dragged him in. She called to him. To them.

"What do you want?" she asked through the closed door.

Her voice was sharp and edged with tension, but it washed over him like manna from heaven, sending goosebumps skittering across his skin.

"Ah, *salut,*" he said. "I'm your new neighbor from down the hall in apartment thirty-five. My brother and I moved in a few weeks ago." What would she think when she realized they were twins? Would it shock her? Excite her, maybe?

He resisted a smile at the clack of keys on a laptop. She was checking the security feed.

Louis gave the peephole his best smile, the one he reserved for women he wanted to charm. Or coax into their bed. "I wanted to introduce myself." Sometimes his charm didn't work. Sometimes it was Pierre's intensity, his dominance.

Her indecision burned through the door. Then the beep of an alarm being turned off and the slide of the deadbolt being pulled back. The door cracked open and dark eyes behind black frames peeked out. His heart pounded in his chest.

He lifted his hand and waved. "Hi, I'm Louis."

The door opened a little further, glossy black hair spilling over her shoulder.

His lungs seized, and his heart pounded so loud he thought he might have a heart attack. The pull toward her was so much stronger now they stood face to face.

His wolf rushed to the surface, clamoring to be free. It took everything he had to hold it in, to keep his canines from punching through his gums and to push back the dark, coarse hair spreading across the back of his neck. Every instinct called for him to swoop her up in his arms, to wipe the wariness from her eyes and kiss the tightness from her lips.

How the fuck had Pierre stopped himself from pressing her up against the wall and smothering her in his scent? It was a good thing he was standing in the corridor where anyone could come along at any moment. That it'd been Pierre, not him, in the elevator. He wasn't one for delayed gratification. That was Pierre's style, not his.

This situation called for patience and subtlety. *Putain*. He wasn't known for either of those.

He took a step toward her. She stiffened. He backed off, and with considerable effort, pulled himself together. "My brother and I are having a few of the neighbors over for a drink on Saturday night. A sort of introduction. We would like you to come."

"I don't—"

"I'm making mojitos and *noix grillées épicées au miel*—how you say—roasted honey spiced nuts." He did a chef's kiss. And because he couldn't help a little teasing, a little sexual innuendo, he added, "You'll want to taste my nuts, I promise you."

She rewarded him with a flare of heat and a quick drop of her gaze to his groin, then a flush of her cheeks. "I'll think about it."

Then she closed the door in his face.

"*Alor*, it's at seven. On Saturday. Apartment thirty-five." He waited, but although she remained behind the door, she didn't respond. "Nice meeting you. Perhaps when you come by on Saturday, you can tell me your name."

Louis sauntered away. As much as one could saunter with the stranglehold his jeans had on his impossibly hard cock. He didn't once glance at the security cameras, but she had to be watching. He smiled. Wary, but interested. Perhaps despite herself, but her scent didn't lie.

Pierre was waiting for him when he entered their apartment, the security feed open on his laptop. "*Alor*? Will she come?"

Louis flopped onto the sofa beside his brother. "I don't know. Maybe. I hope so. I... Pierre, what's happening here?"

Pierre set aside his laptop. "Did you feel it, too?"

"If by feel it you mean the overpowering urge to make her mine...then *oui*, I felt it." He met his brother's gaze, and a certainty settled in his bones. "She's ours."

Pierre growled. "Ours."

"It could be awkward, her working with the enemy."

Pierre sucked in a breath. "*Oui*."

"We charm her while we deceive her."

Pierre grimaced. "Not the best way to start, but it could be worse."

Oui. Maxime was proof of that. Poor *connard*. Though, given this situation, Maxime might not be drinking away his sorrows alone for long. "She *is* our mate. That has to count for something."

Pierre cocked an eyebrow. "Tell that to Maxime."

"There's two of us."

"*Oui*."

It had always been their advantage — working together. Hell, they did everything together — worked, lived, fucked women. This was a dance they knew all too well. But this time, the stakes were higher. Melinda Cheng was no random hookup in a nightclub. A one and done, killing time while they waited for their mate. She *was* their mate.

Louis held out his fist, bumping knuckles with his twin. "She doesn't stand a chance."

Melinda Cheng was theirs, and nothing, no security system, not their mission, or Cordelia King, was going to keep her out of their arms.

Chapter Four

Melinda scanned the street one more time. Nothing. Not a single sighting of Mr. Excalibur or Louis all day. Two days ago, Louis had stood at her door inviting her to their apartment for drinks on Saturday. Tonight. She'd checked the security feed. He hadn't lied when he'd said he'd invited all the neighbors. More than the ones on this floor. Mr. Excalibur had popped up on the security feed, knocking on doors on the floor above and the one below. Maybe they were nothing more than new neighbors being friendly.

Louis' words came back to her. *You'll want to taste my nuts, I promise you.* More than friendly. His cheeky grin as he'd spoken had left no doubt it wasn't an unfortunate mistake because of the language barrier.

She didn't know what had possessed her to open her door. Melinda could've ignored his knocking, pretended she wasn't at home. Perhaps it was the impulse to treat neighbors as family, something her mother had instilled in her since she was old enough to walk. Or the desire to see him in the flesh, face to face. Not the quick glance at his back and glutes she'd caught in the bakery. Or the distorted view of him through the peephole. No. In truth, she was curious. They were identical twins, but how different were they, really?

The more times she viewed the security feed, studying the two men — too many times in the last two days — the more differences she found. Louis, with his loping gait and ready smile, was playful, bouncing to the beat of whatever music he listened to in his ear buds as he hit the stairwell, greeting other tenants with a big grin and an exchange of words. Mr. Excalibur, with his fancy watch and serious expression, strode with purpose, acknowledging others with a brief nod, more reserved than his twin, but his intensity was no less disarming than Louis' boyish charm.

They were a powerhouse pair. Though the security feed was grainy, it hadn't diminished the effect of their taut asses and defined pecs in those snug jeans and fitted black shirts. *Hell.* If she watched any more footage of them, she'd soon be offering to have their babies.

When she wasn't drooling over their black-and-white images going to and from their apartment, she'd been digging into their identities. Trying to establish who these men were, running them through all the software she could think of, and trolling through social media platforms looking for them. She'd even hacked into the online sales data of Roger Dubius, for goodness' sake. Two sleepless nights, hours in front of her screens. Having a name helped, but she'd learned very little. Every morsel hard won. What she'd found would barely justify the file she'd created for it.

Louis and Pierre Montagne. Thirty years old. Unmarried. Residents of Paris, France. Employees of

Wolf Enterprises. The more she dug into Wolf Enterprises, the more convinced she became it was a shadow company, a front. Created for whatever purpose they were in London? Possibly. What they did for this company also remained a mystery.

She'd found a few photos of them on social media — not their platforms, for they had none she could find — looking sexy as hell in designer suits. They had taste *and* money. Never alone, always with women. Beautiful women. Usually sandwiched between the two of them at events, all high-end. Never the same woman twice. Her body lit up every time she looked at those photos, imagining what happened when the cameras were gone.

The implication was clear. These twins liked to share. It wasn't as if she hadn't had that exact thought. Every time she saw them on the security feed. Every time she'd lain in bed, her eyes closed, her hand sliding down her body and into her sleep pants, visualizing them slipping between her sheets.

Was that all they were? Two playboy twins? That they'd purchased an apartment down the hall from her merely a coincidence? Nothing to do with her client?

Her blank screen, the victim of malware, taunted her. She would feel much better if she knew what Wolf Enterprises specialized in. It had a predatory ring about it. Maybe it was an ultra-discreet security firm. Or a private investigator for the wealthy. But had the malware attack come from them, or from someone else?

Melinda rubbed her sternum. She had a bad feeling about all this, and nothing good came from ignoring bad feelings. Her mother had. She'd trusted instead in the matchmakers, the portents, the complimentary horoscopes, and the good family she would marry into and she'd ended up in a living nightmare. Melinda was not going to follow down that road. Not if she had any say in it.

She approached her building with a meal to go from her favorite noodle bar and three tins of jasmine tea, once again on alert. This morning, she'd had a call from the refuge, forcing her out of her apartment. Another woman needed her skills and Melinda couldn't—wouldn't—turn her away. She'd also run out of jasmine tea.

This time she'd taken precautions—switching trains, getting off at a different station and walking a few extra blocks—both on the journey there and on the trip home. Not once had she spotted one of the twins, or anyone else, following her.

Melinda pushed through the entrance doors to an empty foyer. She tapped her foot while the lift took an eternity to return to the ground floor. When the doors opened, she stepped inside and punched the number for her floor. The doors slid closed, then bounced back open again.

Her heart stopped. Two men in familiar snug jeans and black Henleys stepped into the lift.

"We meet again," said Mr. Excalibur—Pierre—taking up position to her right.

Louis stepped to her left as the doors slid closed again. Their bodies loomed beside her, their heady aftershave filling her lungs and eliciting a flurry of goosebumps across her skin. The space closed in and the lift, rated for a maximum of fifteen people, seemed far too small for the three of them.

Louis took an exaggerated sniff of the air. "Mm, something smells good."

His voice rumbled through her, and her foot tap-tapped. She pressed it to the floor to make it stop.

Pierre leaned closer, brushing against her shoulder, and sniffed the air. "*Oui*. Divine."

Melinda flushed and fiddled with her glasses while the elevator trundled slower than dial-up internet.

"What do you have there?" Louis peered into her bag. "Something spicy?"

He gave her one of those high-wattage smiles she'd seen on the security feed, but in person, with him standing so damn close, the effect was a hundred times more powerful. Melinda locked her knees to prevent both feet from jiggling.

"Uhm...shacha noodles with spicy sausage, tofu and vegetables." Melinda almost groaned aloud. *Why didn't I just say noodles? He doesn't need to know my personal preferences.*

"Mmm," Louis rumbled, rocking back and forward on his feet. "I like spicy, don't you, Pierre?"

Unlike his twin, he stood still, his arms crossed, frowning at the control panel. "I thought you lived on the eighth floor?"

The lit button for floor nine blazed away like an accusation. "Oh, the other day. Right. I..." She wracked her brain for a plausible excuse. "I had to visit one of the other tenants on the eighth floor."

Louis swung to face his twin, bringing his pecs right into her line of vision and really, really close. "She lives in apartment thirty-four. Down the hall from us. I've invited her over to taste my nuts tonight." He dropped his gaze to Melinda. "You are coming, no?"

Melinda flushed at the reference to Louis' nuts again as she ogled his chest. So close. Within touching distance. Close enough, if she were to lean forward, she could take a bite.

Oh, God. Did I just…

Melinda took a step back and ran into Pierre.

Pierre placed gentle hands on her shoulders. "*Salut,* neighbor." His breath whispered across her head. "I do hope you will *come* tonight."

Her breathing stuttered and her heart raced. Was she mistaken in hearing the double entendre in his words? Or was it wishful thinking on her part?

Louis hooked a finger under her chin and raised her focus from his pecs to his face. "Going to tell us your name, *chérie*? Seeing as we live down the hall, we should be on a first-name basis."

Melinda opened her mouth, but no sound came out. He rubbed his thumb across her bottom lip, his gaze dipping. He leaned closer.

Is he going to…? Do I want him to? That was a loud hell, yes.

Pierre dropped a hand to her hip and pressed into her from behind. All that taut muscle against her shoulder blades, the heat of his hand through her sweats, the prod of…

The lift ground to a halt, and the door slid open with a whoosh.

Pierre's grip tightened on her hip. "Your name, *mon amour*?"

"Melinda," she blurted out.

"Melinda." Louis smiled, a big, beautiful smile that could light up the world.

It certainly lit up parts of her body.

He dropped his hand and backed out of the lift. "Come join us tonight." He winked. "You won't regret it."

Pierre released her, too, and stepped out of the elevator. He glanced back at her, the heat in his gaze unmistakable. "Until tonight, Melinda."

The elevator doors closed and Melinda stood on legs as wobbly as a bowl of over-cooked noodles. She pressed the button, the door slid open again and she peered out into the corridor. Empty. The door down the hall, closed. With quick steps, she reached her apartment, keyed the lock and slammed her door behind her. She punched in her alarm code and slumped to the floor, her heart still racing.

Manchu trotted over with a soft meow and rubbed against her knee.

"Hey, buddy." She picked him up and cradled him to her, listening to the purr rumble through his chest. "Things would be easier if you were the only man I had to worry about, hm?"

Manchu's amber eyes regarded her.

"These men are trouble, Manchu. But what type of trouble…" She sighed. "I wish I knew."

Chapter Five

Louis had his zipper down and his cock in his hand before he'd cleared the living area. He threw himself on his bed, spread his legs and ran his hand from base to tip, collecting the bead of pre-cum and smearing it over his shaft as he slid his hand down again. *Putain.* He'd wanted to strip her naked, sink to his knees and bury his face in her *minou.*

She hadn't reached for either of them, but she'd wanted to. In that split second before her mind had caught up with her body and caution warred with desire, she'd entertained the thought of having both of them in her bed. It was in the widening of her eyes, the parting of her lips and the blossoming of her sweet scent in the enclosed space of the elevator.

A groan tore from his lips and he thrust into his hand, squeezing his fist around his cock. Oh, to be deep inside her, to have her hands exploring his body. Would she be hesitant? Or would she be bold, losing herself to the passion? As Pierre's olive-skinned hands cupped the golden skin of her small breasts, teasing her nipples to peaks while he dived between her slender thighs?

Would she be bare or natural? Louis didn't care. He flicked his thumb over the tip of his cock, imagining it was her tongue, before doing another long slide down his shaft with his fist as though she'd taken him in that cute little mouth of hers, her dark eyes almost black with her desire.

He quickened his pace, the thought of her glorious wet mouth around him bringing him to the edge faster than he'd thought possible. Hell, an all-night session of debauched sex had never gripped him as hard as the thought of Melinda sucking his cock. Was Pierre as affected? Was she?

Had she slipped into her apartment and torn off her clothes in a desperate need to be naked, to touch herself? To rub her little *bonbon,* tweak her nipples and slide her fingers through her wet heat? Or did she prefer toys? His release sizzled at the base of his spine, his hand pumping furiously. He could have fun with toys. Would she lie on her bed as he had, her head thrown back, or would she watch herself in the mirror, her chest heaving?

His release hit him like a sonic boom, and he all but bowed off the bed as thick ropes of cum spurted across his shirt and hand.

Putain.

His breathing labored, Louis collapsed back on the bed. If that was a hint of what they would experience together… It was almost enough to have him charge down the corridor, break down her door, and throw himself at her feet this very instant.

Louis was on his feet, heading for the door, his shirt a mess and his cock still swinging free, when a moan from the living area pulled him up short. *Pierre.* His brother would crash tackle him to the floor if he tried it. And rightly so. She wasn't ready yet. Melinda might desire them, but she wouldn't be feeling the imperative to mate, to claim, to bite quite like they were. She was human, with no idea his kind existed.

All he would achieve would be to scare her off. Then they'd have to spend more time tracking her down again. That wouldn't do anyone any good. Maxime would be pissed, and Gabriel would have his balls. Louis was rather attached to those.

And the clock was ticking. Charming their mate wasn't their only mission. Cordelia King was still out there.

With that sobering thought, he tossed his soiled shirt into the laundry basket, grabbed a fresh one then cleaned up in the bathroom. He tucked his cock back into his boxers and zipped up his jeans. When he walked into the living room, Pierre sat on the lounge in a similar position he had been in not ten minutes prior—his hard-as-granite cock free of his jeans and his hand wrapped loosely around it, a pinched expression on his face.

"Are you going to take care of that?" He headed for the kitchen, snagged a Red Bull from the refrigerator and threw himself on the hideous sofa beside his twin.

Pierre tucked his cock back into his pants, wincing as he struggled to get the zipper done up. "*Non.*"

Louis cracked the tab on his can and shook his head. "Fuck you and your delayed gratification."

Pierre chuckled. "It'll be worth every moment when we have her in our bed."

"Heads up, brother. When we have her in our bed, I'm not waiting."

"You never do, Louis, but you know that suits me fine."

Oui. They worked well as a team, despite their obvious differences. Louis liked to get into the action right from the start. Pierre preferred to watch for a while before joining in. He said it heightened his pleasure, denying himself while Louis took his fill. Had they not been twins, it probably wouldn't work. They were, and it did. And when Pierre joined in... Louis grinned. No woman had ever complained.

His mood soured. No. They liked it. The idea of two identical men taking them until they could barely walk, leaving them limp and well-sated, with memories no human man could ever live up to. What they weren't interested in was putting in the effort to get to know them as individuals. No woman in their past had ever been able to tell them apart, no matter how much time they spent with them. Even if they wore different clothes. Not a single one.

It frustrated him no end. And Pierre, too. As far as he was concerned, it was as obvious as the bulge in Pierre's jeans. They may be identical twins, but they *were* different. His pack could tell them apart. Any shifter worth their genes could.

Humans could be so blind sometimes. Just once, he would like a woman to spot the differences. To see him as a separate identity. He glanced at Pierre. *Oui*, his twin would like that, too.

"She's our mate, Louis. She'll be different from all the others."

As usual, his brother had picked up on his thoughts. Being twins did have its advantages.

Pierre often had the right of any situation, but this time, Louis wasn't so sure. "What if she's not?"

Would it matter? If she couldn't tell them apart? She was their mate. They would love and cherish her all the same, but... *Oui*. It mattered.

Pierre shrugged. "Then we'll show her. Before we turn her."

Oui, before they turned her. As a werewolf, she couldn't fail to miss the signs, but he wanted his mate to see him as a whole person, not as an extension of his brother, right from the start. He held out his hand and bumped knuckles with his brother.

He took a sip of Red Bull. "What if this doesn't work? What if she doesn't come tonight? What's our next step? We're short on time here, Pierre. Gabriel rang me again this morning. We need to find Cordelia."

"Melinda's spent the last two days hunting us online, finding only what I wanted her to find. An invitation to our apartment is too good an opportunity for her to pass up. She'll come."

Louis' nostrils flared. Their mate in their apartment... Once she crossed that threshold, it was going to be one hell of a challenge to let her leave.

Chapter Six

It'd been four hours since Melinda had been caught in the lift with Louis and Pierre, but every moment of their encounter had lived on replay in her brain ever since. She'd dissected it, rehashed it. It'd fueled her fantasies all afternoon. Erotic fantasies. She'd never experienced such a visceral reaction to a man before. To *two* men.

She leaned on the kitchen bench, her head in her hands as her jasmine tea steeped. Maybe she needed something stronger. To ease the craving, the need that had her clenching her thighs at the mere sight of one of them on the security feed. Footage she'd checked too damn often to be healthy.

Melinda poured her tea and headed back to her screens. Work. That would fix this fascination she had with the twins. Sliding into her chair, she pulled up the tab with her newest client—username JohnnyBeGood. Johnny *hadn't* been good. That was why he needed a new identity. The women at the refuge couldn't pay her for her skills, but Melinda was good at what she did so she could charge her *other* clients a lot of money. Clients like JohnnyBeGood.

On another screen, movement on the security feed caught her eye. A couple from the eighth floor — Tom and Jacob — stepped from the lift, and she followed them from camera to camera as they passed her door and stopped at apartment thirty-five. She checked the time. Six-fifty-eight. The door opened and Pierre, in black jeans and collared black shirt, the top few buttons undone to reveal a hint of dark chest hair, appeared. Melinda leaned closer. Pierre gave the couple a rare smile and beckoned them inside. He paused in the doorway and looked straight up at the camera. At her.

Melinda gasped and sat back, though she knew it was ridiculous. He couldn't see her. He couldn't possibly know she was watching. *Could he?* Pierre stood there, long seconds passing. With a bite of his bottom lip that had her melting into her panties, he retreated inside and closed the door.

Her dark monitor, the one that had flashed its warning of a security breach, taunted her. That bad feeling was back again, stronger than ever. Was it time to warn her client? Send a message to MysticMage?

Melinda logged into her IRC channel, found the thread she was after and typed up a brief message to the woman about a possible compromise to her new identity. She hovered her fingers over the keys, uncertain. This was no time to be coy. She typed one last sentence, asking if her client had any connections in France, and if the names Montagne or Wolf Enterprises meant anything to her.

Her finger poised over the enter key, she glanced at the security feed. The lift opened again, spilling out more guests. A young lawyer from the floor above, still dressed in her power suit, and an older couple, home on a rare break from cruising the Mediterranean. This time it was Louis who opened the door, his hair appealingly ruffled and an old lady's floral apron unashamedly wrapped around his waist.

As with Pierre, after the guests had disappeared inside, he paused and looked directly at the camera. He grinned at her, his trademark smile. She watched the screen, enthralled. Then he winked. Melinda nearly fell off her chair.

They *knew*. That she was watching them through the security feeds. *Who* are *these men?*

There was one sure way to find out. It might be unimaginably stupid, and her mother had always complained she had too much tiger in her, but an invitation into their apartment wasn't an opportunity she should waste. She could spend days, weeks — maybe more — digging into Wolf Enterprises, hacking their devices, but one quick snoop through their apartment could give her all the information — and the access — she needed. Then she'd know exactly why they were here.

Decision made, she hit send on her message, then changed into something more appropriate for a party. If it was a little more feminine than her day-to-day wear, if she fussed over her hair a little too long, added lip gloss she hadn't worn in months, it was because she wanted to fit in with the other guests. Not because she was trying to impress two hot-as-Hades twins.

Melinda slung a purse over her shoulder with her keys, her phone and a thumb drive loaded with a few programs she could use to access any tech she found. As an afterthought, she grabbed a second thumb drive she'd uploaded with a gorgeous little virus she'd come across a couple of months ago. If she found anything incriminating, if they were up to something nefarious involving her, she could use it to destroy their operating systems with a few keystrokes. She would have liked to take a laptop with her, but she doubted she could sneak that in undetected. With a quick rub on Manchu's head, she set her alarms then headed down the corridor to apartment thirty-five.

Pierre answered the door, the hint of a smirk on his lips as he led her into the living area. "I'm glad you came, Melinda. Drink? Beer? Wine? A mojito?"

She had no plans to drink too much. She was here for one thing and one thing only, but it would be odd for her not to at least have one. "White wine will be fine, thank you."

She did a quick scan of the entry. No security system on the door. Interesting, and a little surprising. They were confident. Or they had nothing to hide. From the looks of the hideous floral sofa, dusky rose drapes and crocheted doilies, nothing else had changed since Mrs. Bellamy had moved out either.

"Interesting décor," she said. "Not what I expected."

Pierre handed her a glass of wine. "Louis and I haven't come to a consensus on that yet."

Or they didn't plan to stay long.

Louis extricated himself from the attentions of the lawyer and headed her way, snatching up a tray with dip, crisps, olives, figs and roasted walnuts.

"*Salut*, Melinda. You came." He held the tray out to her. "You must try my roasted nuts. I added a little extra spice. Just for you. You like it spicy, no?"

The challenge in his eyes was too much to resist. She took a couple of walnuts and slipped one in her mouth, making a show of biting down on it. Louis' nostrils flared, Pierre edged a little closer.

Flavor burst on her tongue. *Oh, my God.* It was amazing. The crunch of the walnut, the sweetness of the honey, and the bite of heat from the chili. Melinda popped another one into her mouth, forgetting herself for a moment, closing her eyes and letting out a little moan.

"Is good, no?"

Melinda snapped her eyes open to Louis' intense focus on her mouth. She took a sip of wine, hiding her flush and nodded. "Yes. They're good."

Louis beamed. "I knew you would like my nuts." He nudged his brother. "She likes my nuts, Pierre."

She tossed a few more into her mouth. This time, she kept her eyes open, and it was the fierce intensity, the held breaths of both twins that had her wanting to moan. She swallowed and licked her lips. They tracked the motion.

"Louis, Pierre." Tom from the floor below broke their little bubble. "Please tell me you're going to do something with this apartment. Change the drapes, maybe burn that sofa. I know of a good designer, if you're interested."

Melinda seized the opportunity to move away, mingling with the other guests. She circled, smiling and chatting, scoping out the room. No laptops, no phones. Nothing. Not a single personal item, nor anything that might hint at what they did for work. What Wolf Enterprises specialized in. The whole time, the burn of twin gazes followed her.

She ducked into the kitchen. A quick glance told her she wouldn't find what she was searching for here. When she returned to the living area, both Louis and

Pierre were watching, waiting for her. Because they were hoping for something from her later, or because they were suspicious?

Melinda mingled, spending more time on small talk with her neighbors than she had in all the years she'd lived in her building. After Joe from across the hall had regaled her with tales of his successes in the advertising world for far too long, Melinda set her glass down on the coffee table, made her excuses and headed down the hall to the bathroom. In case anyone — Pierre or Louis specifically — happened to be watching, she did use the bathroom. She checked the vanity cupboard, not expecting to find anything out of the ordinary. Rolls of toilet paper, some shaving gear, a tube of toothpaste and toothbrushes — one neat and trim, the other shaggy. Pierre and Louis. Twins they may be, but their personalities shone through.

She eased open the door and peeked out. Down the corridor, in the living area, people chatted. Louis had his back to her, deep in animated conversation with Mr. Patel. His hands moved as he talked, his whole body invested, as boisterous as his personality. Pierre stood with a guy from the floor above, one hand tucked in his pocket, the other cradling a glass of red wine, a brief nod of agreement at something the guy said.

With light steps, Melinda ducked out of the bathroom and into the second bedroom. She sucked in the hint of aftershave, and something else, something musky but not unpleasant. It had her nipples pebbling and her panties dampening. As her eyes adjusted to the meager light of the numerals on an old alarm clock, she could make out the unmade bed still bearing the imprint of a large male body, the floral duvet thrust back. Louis? An image of him naked, sheets twisted about his calves, his hand wrapped around his cock, flashed into her mind. Heat suffused her face.

She should turn around. Retreat to the safety of the living room.

No. These men are up to something, and I need to know what it is.

She slammed a lid on her imagination and her libido, pulled out her phone, switched on the flashlight and turned to the open closet.

An overnight bag sat in the bottom, open, clothes spewing out. She riffled through it, her hand lingering on a pair of soft black boxer briefs. Louis would fill these out nicely. She thrust them aside and rooted through the rest of the clothes, mostly black. What was it with these men and black? Was it some kind of uniform? A reflection of their work? Black Ops? She checked the pockets of the bag. Nothing. She ran her hands along the top shelf of the closet. No laptop.

Putting everything back as she'd found it, she abandoned the closet and checked the rest of the room. Nothing. She peered out into the hallway. No one was looking her way. She slipped into the other bedroom, the main bedroom. Oh, this one definitely belonged to Pierre. The bed was made, the closet was empty except for a neatly stored overnight bag, and his clothes — again almost all black — he'd folded neatly in the dresser. She sucked in a breath. No boxer briefs. No underwear of any kind. The man went commando. All buttoned up on the outside, free underneath. She pulled out a pair of gray sweatpants.

Commando *and* gray sweatpants.

She slammed the drawer shut. For goodness' sake, she was almost panting.

Melinda checked the remaining drawers. No sign of a laptop or a phone. She checked under the bed, under the pillows, under the mattress, careful to smooth out the duvet. Nothing in the drawers of the bedside tables. It stood to reason they would have their phones on them, but they'd both arrived with laptop bags, so where was their tech? And why were they hiding it?

"Melinda?"

Shit.

She shoved her phone back in her purse and slowly turned around. Pierre leaned against the door frame, silhouetted by the light in the hall. By his side, Louis.

Chapter Seven

Pierre sucked in a breath. She was in *his* room, standing before *his* bed, and didn't that make his cock hard as fuck. He'd been borderline hard from the moment he'd opened the door to her. Her V-neck sweater revealing the gentle swell of her breasts. The sway of her slender hips in her jeans. The gloss of her lips an invitation to taste. That little moan when she'd eaten Louis' honey roasted chili walnuts.

He'd spent his nights with his whole body focused on her, imagining her staring at her screens as she swam in cyberspace trying to pin them down. A gentle touch of code here, a poke there. She was good, but he and Louis were better, and they'd fed her just enough to whet her appetite. Enough to have her take up their invitation. And now here she was, so close to his bed that his brain struggled to think of anything else but her in it, naked, sandwiched between the two of them.

Had she lain in bed at night fantasizing about both of them taking her? He knew he had. So had Louis. If his hearing hadn't betrayed him, Louis had jerked himself raw over the idea. Not him. His body rippled with his need, exquisite sexual tension gripping his balls tight, all but exploding with his desperation for release. Soon. With her. In her. And it would be all the more powerful, sublime, for the wait.

Louis bounced on the balls of his feet, the musk of his wolf strong in the air.

"Patience," Pierre whispered, barely loud enough for Louis to hear him.

Louis mimed a groan.

Oui, the pull to go to her, snatch her up and toss her on the bed was strong. Stronger than anything he'd ever experienced. He breathed in, letting the delicious sensation wash over him, reveled in it. *Putain*, he could almost come with it alone.

"I..." Melinda ducked her head, letting her hair fall across her face. She seemed to collect herself, raising her chin, flicking her gaze between the two of them. "I'm sorry. I didn't mean to invade your privacy. It's just..."

Pierre stepped into the room.

"The...um...furnishings in the living area were just so *bad* I had to see if they were the same throughout." There was a nervousness to her chuckle. "I mean, two grown men sleeping in beds all pink and floral."

Pierre took another step toward her, and she retreated, the back of her knees hitting the bed. "With the lights off?"

"Well, I...ah..."

"I think," said Louis, closing the door behind him, plunging them into darkness, "Melinda might want to skip all the festivities and small talk and go straight for the finale of the evening. What do you say, Pierre? Are you ready for dessert?"

A growl rumbled up in his chest. Melinda's eyes widened, and her glossy mouth parted on a gasp. With the door closed, she'd be all but blind. But they weren't, and the vision before him, looking more appetizing than any dessert he'd ever had, called to him. *Oui*, he was all in with Louis' idea.

Louis, ever impatient, was across the room before he could stop him. "How do you want to play this, Pierre? Both together? You first? Or shall I bend her over your bed while you watch?"

A catch of breath, a swallow, a clenching of her thighs, the slight arch of her back and the unmistakable scent of a woman aroused. It coated his tongue and soaked into his lungs. Not just any woman. Theirs. There was no better fragrance in the world.

He closed the distance between them, and any thought of finding Cordelia, or why Melinda had truly come to their apartment, or was in his bedroom, vanished as her heady fragrance surrounded him and shot the small amount of remaining blood in his brain straight to his dick. Everything but his primal urge to mate ceased to exist.

Melinda's hands fluttered about, her eyes searching the darkness. "I...we...should return to the party."

Pierre cupped her cheek, and she jumped, her heart rate spiking. "Too late for that, *mon amour*."

"But...your other guests...we..."

"Shh." Louis planted a finger on her lips, and her breath hitched. He plucked her little bag off her shoulder and dropped it to the ground, then slipped her glasses from her face, placing them on top of the chest of drawers.

Pierre slid his hand from her cheek to her nape, pulling her in close. A shiver rippled through her body, so slight he might have missed it had he not been what he was. He hovered his lips above hers, their breaths mingling, waiting for a refusal, a denial. Eyes wide and her pulse an erratic beat in her throat, she remained silent. But when she leaned into him, the message from her body was loud and clear. Pierre ducked his head and slanted his mouth across hers. Her small hands gripped at his shirt and her tongue slipped out to play.

He groaned into her mouth. Never had a kiss been so devastating. It made his heart race. It made him weak at the knees. His wolf wanted to howl his triumph. Over a kiss. A simple kiss.

Louis nudged his shoulder. "I want to taste her, too."

Pierre released her lips, satisfied at the glazed look in her eyes. Louis turned her head his way, and fuck, wasn't it all kinds of hot watching his twin devour her mouth, too? She released one hand from his shirt and grabbed hold of Louis'.

Forget their party and their other guests. And Cordelia. Nothing was more important than satisfying their mate. He nudged her backward, and the three of them toppled onto the bed, Louis at her side and him braced above her, one knee between her thighs.

"She's wearing too many clothes, Pierre."

He grunted his agreement, and as Louis dragged her sweater up, revealing her lacy white *soutien-gorge* and the hint of dusky nipples poking through, he popped the button on her jeans.

Melinda's gaze flicked to the door. "What if — "

He silenced her with a kiss, rolling onto his side, taking her with him, bracketing her between the two of them. She moaned into his mouth as Louis slipped a hand between them and cupped her breast, tweaking her nipple. She didn't protest when he dragged her zipper down and slid his hand inside her jeans. Melinda moaned again and thrust her hips as his fingers brushed against the damp patch on her panties.

"So wet for us, *mon amour*," he murmured against her lips.

With one arm curled around his neck, and another around Louis', she held them close with a strength born of passion. Their little mate was all in and it had him wanting to rip her clothes off and sink his cock into her wet heat. Right. Now.

He surfaced for a minute, and caught Louis, canines extended, hovering over the curve of her neck. Pierre snarled, and their hot little mate whimpered and pressed against his palm. He glared at Louis until his twin retracted his teeth. "Not yet. Not now. Melinda needs to come."

Yes! She needed to come. With Louis at her back, his hand on her breast, his lips at her throat and the steel bar of his erection pressed against her ass, and Pierre slipping his hand inside her knickers... Melinda gasped and gave a roll of her hips, chasing it. The man was as good with his mouth as he was with his fingers. Circling her clit, stroking his fingers through her slick folds. It was almost embarrassing how wet she was.

They surrounded her. Twin muscular bodies pressed against her, the heady fragrance of their aftershave and something musky and male. Both with their hands on her, both kissing her. It was overwhelming. It was...

Pierre slipped a finger inside her, his thumb pressing against her clit. She threw her head back onto Louis' shoulder, pushing her breast more firmly into his palm. He took advantage, rolling her already peaked nipple between his fingers. The sounds that spilled from her mouth were obscene, but she couldn't help it. To be the focus of both twins' devotion to her body unraveled something within her. Brought out the inner deviant in her she hadn't known existed.

Louis chuckled. "Hush, my little *pirate informatique*. We don't want the whole apartment to hear."

Pierre growled again, the sound reverberating in his chest, and she clenched around his finger.

Again the chuckle in her ear. "I think she likes it when you growl, Pierre."

Pierre slipped another finger inside her, stretching her, a slow delicious slide in and out and back in again. Then he growled again. Heat swirled through her, and she clenched around Pierre's hand as she hovered on the edge of what she suspected would be the most momentous orgasm she'd ever had in her entire life.

Louis slipped two fingers into her mouth. "Suck, *bébé*."

And she did, tasting Louis, riding Pierre. She bit down on Louis' fingers, convinced she might spontaneously combust.

"Our little Melinda has teeth, Pierre."

The clack of heels down the corridor, and a door closing, brought sanity back with a kick.

Oh, God. What am I doing? What are they *doing?* There were a bunch of her neighbors out there, probably wondering where their hosts had gone. And here she was, getting down and dirty. With both of them.

Melinda wrenched Louis' fingers from her mouth and pushed at Pierre, shoving him onto his back, his fingers sliding free. Tugging down her sweater, Melinda scrambled off the bed and zipped up her jeans. "I...I didn't mean for..."

The toilet flushed. A faucet turned on, turned off again. A door opened and the clack of heels retreated toward the living room.

"I have to go." Her body was on fire, but she ignored it, searching the floor in the dark, finding her purse and snatching it up.

She felt around for her glasses, kicked her shin on the bed, then found them on the chest of drawers. Ignoring the throbbing of her shin, she smoothed her hair down and set her glasses in place. "Thanks for..." She waved her hand in the air, indicating the drink, the food, the mind-blowing orgasm she'd almost had.

She cracked the door open, a sliver of light landing on the bed. Neither Pierre nor Louis had moved. Pierre put his fingers in his mouth. The two fingers he'd had inside her. He held her gaze as he sucked on them.

A guttural groan from Louis. "I bet she tastes good."

A rumble of agreement from Pierre.

Hell.

Melinda flung open the door and raced down the corridor before she gave in to the demands of her body and did something stupid. Like throw herself back on their bed and at their mercy.

She said hasty goodbyes to her neighbors, begging an early morning start, ignoring a few raised eyebrows, and fled the twins' apartment before either of them surfaced from the bedroom. Sucking in deep lungfuls of air not tainted by aftershave and hot male, she let herself into her apartment, punched in her alarm code and shut the door. But she couldn't close out the memory of what had transpired, nor the unquenched need coursing through her body.

She threw her purse on the sofa and stumbled to her bathroom, splashed cold water on her face, and stared at her flushed reflection in the mirror.

What was I thinking?

She'd accepted their invitation for a *reason*. To find something — a laptop, a phone, or any other evidence — that would clue her in on what the twins were up to. What they were doing here in London. In this building. Instead… She clenched her thighs. There was no doubt in her mind sex with one — or both — twins, would rock her world. And distract her from her concerns. Had that been their intention? Or had they merely taken advantage of finding her alone and in Pierre's bedroom?

She dried her face and slapped the hand towel down on the vanity. Well, she'd not found a single piece of their tech. She'd not found out anything. That left her no more informed than she had been when she'd left her apartment.

Melinda had two choices. Take care of her current situation with battery operated relief, or channel her pent-up energy into something that might be useful. She grabbed her phone, let herself into her office and booted up her screens. On the security feed, all was quiet. She checked her chat channel. No response from her client.

Her lack of results in the apartment meant she was doing this the cyber way. She should've done it in the first place. She was getting sloppy.

Her dark screen mocked her. She should get started on that, too.

Melinda set to work. The way her body was humming, she wouldn't be sleeping. If she found something incriminating, if the twins were responsible for the malware? Manchu jumped onto her lap, butting his head against her chin. Then she'd take Manchu and run. Warn her client, and hunker down somewhere. Give herself a new identity. Start again. She'd done it once. With her mother gone, there'd been no reason to stay at home. She was older now, more experienced. And this time, she wouldn't be starting with nothing.

If the malware came from someone else? If the twins were nothing more sinister than new neighbors? Her body lit up at the memory of their mouths, their hands on her. Melinda checked the security feed. Guests were leaving the party. Pierre stood in the doorway with Mr. Patel. The old man said his goodbyes, crossed the hall and disappeared into his apartment. Louis joined Pierre, leaning on the door frame. They both looked up, staring straight at the camera. Straight at her. Melinda caught her breath and held it, unable to look away. How she wanted it to *not* be them. Her body especially. But they were too aware of the security cameras for them to not be up to something. Aware like she was. Like a hacker.

Melinda turned off the screen with the security feed, blanking out the distraction. She had work to do. She was going to crack their hidden SSID, find their IP address and dig into Wolf Enterprises. Pin these men down. Melinda would have her answers. When she was done, she'd know everything there was to know about them, right down to their shoe size.

It was an hour later, deep into her search, that Melinda remembered Louis' words.

"Hush, my little pirate informatique. We don't want the neighbors to hear."

Pirate informatique. She didn't speak French, but it didn't take a genius to figure it out. Had she misunderstood? Misheard? She didn't think so. Pierre had growled at Louis, annoyed. It was a slip of the tongue. Something he'd said in the heat of the moment.

They knew she was a hacker.

Chapter Eight

Melinda jerked awake, blinking, the imprint of her keyboard on her cheek. Yawning and stretching, she checked the time on her phone. Three a.m. She'd fallen asleep working at her computers. Manchu had long since abandoned her for somewhere more comfortable — most likely the sofa or her bed — and her tea had gone cold. She logged back into her screens. The twins, so far, were evading her. Maybe she was losing her touch.

The screen with the security feed remained blank, and she resisted the urge to turn it back on, to review the footage of Louis and Pierre. Pierre's smug smile, Louis' wink. Their taut asses. She checked for messages. No response from her client. Had MysticMage not read it yet? She did the calculations in her head. With the time difference, it should be about seven Saturday evening in San Francisco.

MysticMage wasn't as smart as she thought she was. Many dark web users weren't. Maybe she was a first-time user. Melinda wasn't, and it never hurt to know as much about a client as you could. Such information could come in handy. What a woman living in San Francisco wanted with a British identity wasn't for her to question. Perhaps she was planning to flee the States.

An unfamiliar noise had her snapping her attention toward the door. Manchu? Melinda froze. There it was again. What *was* that? She switched on the screen with her security feed. A blank screen greeted her. Tension skittered across the back of her neck. Softly tapping on the keyboard, she brought up the security log. Ten minutes ago, the feed had stopped. Melinda had lived in this building for three years. Not once had this happened. Someone had cut the feed. Someone was in the building, and they didn't want their faces on camera.

She checked her phone. No notifications her alarm was down. It was closed circuit. Nothing wireless for her. She knew how easily they could be hacked. If someone had tried to cut the wires, the backup battery would have kicked in, and a notification would've been sent to her phone.

She checked her phone again. Nothing. *Wait.* Her lungs seized. *No signal. Shit.* They'd jammed the signal.

Another noise, coming from her living room. Someone was in her apartment. The twins?

Galvanized into action, Melinda was out of her chair, tiptoeing to the open door of her office and pressing it closed, wincing at the click as she engaged the deadlock. She debated resetting the alarm. They'd breached the one on her front door. They could do the same with this one. She set it anyway, the small beeps loud in the silence. If they weren't expecting a second alarm, if they tripped it, it would wake all her neighbors on this floor, including Mr. Patel.

With a flick of the light switch, the room darkened, the only light coming from her screens. No time to turn them off, or rip out her hard drives. She grabbed her laptop. There were only so many places in here she could hide. She ducked into the small built-in wardrobe, pushing behind her winter coats, and slid the door shut, leaving it open a bare sliver, and waited, her hands shaking and her whole body on high alert.

She'd been here before, many times. The angry voice of her father and the desperate pleas of her mother echoed in her memories. The closet had been smaller. So had she. But the terror was the same. That help would come too late. She flipped her laptop open, adjusting the brightness of the screen. Her fingers hovered over the keyboard. Back then, she'd called the police. She couldn't do that now. Not with the evidence they'd find on her computers.

Ambulance? Firefighters? They'd bring the police, too. Joe, the advertising guy across the hall? Never had Melinda regretted the solitary life she'd chosen. She did now.

The door knob squeaked, but the door didn't open.

God, she hoped Manchu was okay. That he'd hid under her bed, or behind the sofa.

The knob jiggled again, louder this time. Whoever it was had to know she was in here. A thud hit the door, a shoulder or a boot—all attempts at stealth gone. The door shuddered, but didn't open. They weren't even going to bother with picking the lock this time. Another thud. The wood splintered and the door burst open, slamming against the wall. A piercing wail ripped through the air, followed by loud cursing. In English.

With a British accent. Not the twins. Her relief was short-lived as a large figure silhouetted by the blueish light of her screens moved in front of the cupboard door. If not the twins, then who the hell was in her apartment?

Melinda closed her laptop and shrank back into the corner of the built-in. A loud crashing and banging had her cringing. Her screens? Her computers? This was no burglar. This was a deliberate attack on her and the knowledge she had stored on her hard drives. About one of her clients? The *damn* malware.

MysticMage. *Oh, God.* Melinda hoped she was safe. That she'd received her warning in time.

Over the wail of her alarm, the sounds of destruction went on. Melinda wanted to close her eyes and put her hands over her ears, like she'd done as a child, and cower until it was all over. She clutched her laptop to her chest, resisting the impulse.

The closet door slid open. A brush of cool air and then a beam of red flickered up her chest, over her chin and settled above her eyes.

This was not her father she was hiding from, and the police weren't coming to save her. No one was.

* * * *

Louis collided with Pierre in the living room, the wail of an alarm blaring through the building, almost loud enough to make his ears bleed.

Melinda.

Pierre tossed him a pair of gray sweats. "Pants on."

He stumbled into the sweats and headed for the door.

His twin grabbed his arm, pulling him up short. "Get a hold of yourself."

He snarled at his brother, but Pierre's grip was firm.

"Louis, stop. Others will have heard the alarm. You can't barge out there half-shifted. Someone will see you."

He glanced down at the dark hair creeping across his bare chest, and the claws punching through the tips of his fingers. Pierre was right. He pushed his wolf down deep, ignoring its fury that someone may be hurting his mate. Their mate.

Signs of his beast retreated. "Let's go."

He yanked their door open. He caught the scent of Mr. Patel behind his closed door, too frightened to open it. It wasn't his alarm. Louis raced down the corridor. Joe, from apartment thirty-three, stood in his doorway looking pale and unnerved in a pair of spotty boxers. There was only one other apartment on this floor.

"Get back inside, Joe, and shut the door. We'll deal with this."

"Shall I call the police?"

"No," he snapped.

"We'll take care of it.," said Pierre from behind him. "It's probably a false alarm."

Louis didn't stick around to watch the guy retreat into his apartment. He was at Melinda's door, pushing it open. The deadbolt had been picked, and someone with a lot of expertise had disabled the alarm, maybe even jammed the cell signal. Skilled, but not good enough. They'd not known about the second alarm.

Louis, with Pierre hot on his heels, tracked the scent of an unfamiliar male and the distinctive odor of gun oil through Melinda's apartment, the darkness no hindrance to his enhanced vision. In the doorway to the second bedroom, Melinda's fear hit him with the force of a freight train. Her whimpered pleas sent daggers of ice into his entrails.

Louis barreled into the armed figure standing in front of the built-in closet before the intruder had even clocked his presence. There was a muzzle flash and a pop of air as the gun went off and he slammed the man into the wall. Rage like he'd never before experienced gripped his wolf.

If his shot was true... If he'd hurt Melinda...

Another muzzle flash and Louis couldn't hold his wolf back. He part shifted, the fear in his prey's eyes gratifying, his weak struggles to free himself from Louis' grip useless. Before the shooter could make a sound, he lunged, ripping through the man's throat with his teeth as easily as he would a croissant. A gurgle and the coppery taste of blood in his mouth had Louis wanting to howl his triumph. He contained himself and dropped the dying man to the floor. Heels beat a muted staccato on the carpet and hands clutched at a ruined throat, but it was too late. The intruder's life force was draining out.

Melinda scrambled for the door, screaming and sobbing. Pierre scooped her up, wrapping her in his arms and pressing her face against his chest. Louis leaned into the closet, pulled the cover off the control panel hidden there and ripped out the backup battery.

Blessed silence descended, except for Melinda's soft sobs and Pierre's soothing reassurances they were here now. That she was safe.

"*Putain*, Louis."

Louis turned to his brother. "Is she hurt?"

"The shots went wide, but..." He glared at the body on the floor. "For *fuck's* sake. This is a mess. Clean yourself up. I'll take Melinda back to our place and call Gabriel."

Louis stared at the body of the intruder. Yes, it was a mess. No doubt Joe with the spotty boxers and the skinny white legs would have called the police, but Louis wasn't sorry. The man had broken into Melinda's apartment intending to kill her. If he had his chance over again, he wouldn't hesitate to make the same decision.

Louis kneeled beside the man. Who was he? Why was he here? With night-vision goggles and a Nighthawk pistol, he wasn't your average burglar. He took in the room, the mess of screens and computer towers. A burglar wouldn't have destroyed Melinda's computers, either.

Louis dug through the dead man's pockets. Nothing. No wallet, no keys. Either he had used the Tube, or he had a driver waiting on the street. Not good. He ripped off the night-vision goggles. He didn't recognize the man. If he'd cased the building, he'd been discreet.

Well-equipped *and* highly trained.

Louis leaned closer, spotting the edge of a visible tattoo on the side of the man's neck. He tugged at the shirt collar, pulling it away to reveal a familiar image. Louis gritted his teeth. An F, decorative and adorned with crossed swords.

Fucking Faucherians.

Chapter Nine

Pierre sat on the hideous sofa in their apartment, their mate in his arms, her body shaking. Pressed between them was her laptop. The key to finding Cordelia. But all he could think about right now was that someone had tried to kill his mate. Had nearly succeeded. As fucked up as this situation was, as the scene was in Melinda's second bedroom, he couldn't fault Louis. Had they been a split second later, they would've been too late. Louis had saved Melinda's life.

Louis, once again human, the blood cleaned from his face and chest, strode into their apartment. One look at his tight expression told Pierre the situation was about to get worse.

"Faucherians," Louis mouthed at him.

Faucherians? How? Why? Was Louis sure?

Louis pointed to his neck. *Oui*, Louis was certain. They'd all seen the neck tattoo one too many times to mistake it. Faucherians. A vigilante group who followed the writings of Faucher, a tenth-century *eveque* who'd made it his life's mission to track down and destroy anything supernatural—witches, demons, werewolves. And he'd had a special kind of fervor for the Langeais wolves. His followers were fanatical zealots. In eleven centuries, their obsession with wiping out the Langeais wolves had only intensified. Dedicated, well trained and well supplied, they were more than a thorn in the side of the Langeais wolves.

But what did the Faucherians want with Melinda?

He left their mate in Louis' care and stepped out of their apartment into the quiet corridor. No sign of the police. Yet. He put a call through to Gabriel, the Langeais wolves' head of security and their older brother. Pierre had to get this mess cleaned up before the emergency services arrived. With any luck, since the siren had stopped, they'd treat the call as a false alarm and take their time getting here.

The call rang out. *Merde, Gabriel. Answer your damn phone.* Ever since he'd mated Annabelle, Gabriel was hard to get a hold of. Pierre called again, and he would keep calling until his brother answered.

Gabriel answered the phone with a grunt. "This better be important, Pierre. I'm busy."

A feminine giggle echoed over the phone line. Annabelle. He didn't need two guesses to know what his brother had been up to.

"Well, unbusy yourself. We've got a problem." Pacing, he outlined the situation as quickly as he could.

"Are you sure it was a Faucherian?" Gabriel groaned. "I feel like an *imbecile* every time I say that word."

Oui, it was a stupid name for stupid, bigoted people. Unfortunately, as each century had passed, they'd grown larger and more influential, adding some wealthy and powerful people to their ranks.

"We're sure. We don't know why they targeted Melinda. Maybe because of us?"

"She's the cipher working for Cordelia, no?"

"*Oui.*"

A weighted sigh from Gabriel. "Cordelia's working with the Faucherians."

"What the *fuck*?"

"*Oui,* it surprised me, too, but the Faucherians will do just about anything to destroy us, even, it appears, work with a time-traveling witch."

"Melinda wasn't easy for *us* to find? How did they? I don't believe they have anyone that good."

"You're assuming she didn't tell Cordelia herself."

"I don't think so." A hacker who created new identities for people, some deserving, some not, all desperate, wouldn't advertise where they live.

"There is the possibility…" Gabriel trailed off and there was weight in his silence.

"What, Gabriel? The possibility of what?"

"We, that is Maxime and I, think they might have infiltrated the DGSE."

The Directorate-General for External Security, France's foreign intelligence agency? That changed things. With government resources at their disposal, almost anything was possible.

Annabelle's voice floated across the phone, asking if everything was all right.

"It's Pierre. There's trouble in London," Gabriel replied to her. To Pierre he said, "I'll call Laurent. Have him do clean up. Hopefully, he can get there before the police do. If not, maybe he can run interference. The important thing is, you get the information out of the cipher about Cordelia. We *need* it."

"Melinda. The cipher's name is Melinda."

"Pierre." The warning in Gabriel's voice was clear. "There's no time to fuck around. We need to get Isobella back to the tenth century. We can't put it off much longer, and I sure as hell don't want Cordelia, any of her minions, or the Faucherians showing up to interfere."

"It's not that simple, Gabriel," he ground out through gritted teeth.

"It *fucking* is. If we don't get Isobella back to the tenth century soon, we won't exist. I don't know about you, but I'm pretty attached to my life. Especially now I have Annabelle."

Oui, he understood the urgency. It tugged at him, too. Isobella's destiny was to be the mate of his tenth-century ancestors, Edmond and Aubert Montagne. She was their many times great grandmother. The consequences of her *not* going, he couldn't bear thinking about, but... "She's our mate, Gabriel. Melinda is our mate."

His phone went silent for a moment. "*Merde.* That changes things."

"*Oui.*"

"*D'accord.* Keep me informed. Whatever you do, wherever you go, I want to know about it. And whatever you need, it's yours. We'll work this out."

The tension eased from Pierre's shoulders. "*Merci,* brother."

He ended the call. One thing for certain, they couldn't stay here. The Faucherians had plenty of soldiers. This one may have failed, but the next one they sent might not.

He itched to return to his mate, but there was something he needed to do first. In Melinda's apartment, he snatched a tea towel from a hook in the kitchen, wrapped it around his hand and grabbed a knife. From beneath the sink, he took a bottle of cleaning fluid.

Blood was already congealing on the body as Pierre entered the second bedroom. As Louis had said, the tattoo on the dead man's neck confirmed him as a Faucherian. *Connards.* But he didn't have time to dwell on all the trouble they caused his kind.

Melinda's screens lay on the floor, all of them dark and all smashed. The towers each had several bullet holes in them. Had Cordelia sent the Faucherians to destroy any evidence Melinda might have? Including Melinda herself? If so, what had prompted her to send them now?

His gums throbbed and his canines threatened to punch through, but he resisted the pull of his wolf. He must be certain the dead man had done the job. If someone discovered the body before Laurent could get here, it wouldn't take long for the police to pull the footage from the security cameras which, along with Melinda's computers, would be taken in as evidence.

The security logs in the building were easy enough to wipe, to hide their presence over the last few weeks. He'd have to get onto that soon, but there was still Melinda's feed in her flat to contend with. There was no camera in this room, and no recording of Louis' part shift when he killed the Faucherian — thank fuck — but there would be of them entering the apartment. Who knew what other incriminating information she might have on her hard drives? Things about her clients and what she did for a living that Melinda wouldn't want discovered.

Using the tea towel to prevent leaving prints, he ripped off the casings of all four towers, located the hard drives in each of them and plunged the knife through them multiple times, just to be sure. Satisfied his destruction would render them in operable, he tucked her phone into his pocket and using the cleaning fluid, wiped down the alarm cover and battery, removing any print or DNA Louis might have left behind.

In her bedroom, still using the tea towel, he dug around in her closet for an overnight bag, and tossed a few clothes in it. She couldn't stay here. Not anymore. From her dresser, he selected under garments — plain and utilitarian, except for a set of barely there red lace. He fingered the material, imagining her in nothing but these, then shoved them in the bag. With any luck, he might get to see them on her.

In her bedside drawer, her passport — in the name of Mei Lin Lee — and... *Putain.* He stared at the small, purple, egg-shaped vibrator with a curling tail and the matching remote. Before he could second guess his decision, he snatched up the vibrator and its remote and slipped them into the pocket of his sweats. Her passport went into the bag, as did her phone.

A noise from beneath the bed had him freezing. He sniffed the air. Feline. Melinda's cat. From the hours of footage they'd watched of Melinda, she had an attachment to her furry companion. *Merde.*

He found two shopping bags under the sink and filled them with tins of cat food, cat bowls, a bag of cat litter and the litter tray from the bathroom after emptying it onto the floor. The ginger tabby put up a hell of a fight, yowling, scratching and biting as he grabbed it by the scruff, hauled it out from under Melinda's bed and shoved it in the cat carrier he'd found on top of the water heater in the bathroom. The cat knew he was a predator, even if Melinda didn't.

As an afterthought, he grabbed Melinda's teapot, which he wrapped in a clean tea towel, and her tins of jasmine tea, and loaded them into the shopping bag with the cat supplies. After tonight, she was going to need her tea. He snatched her purse off the sofa and shoved the tea towel in the shopping bag. Pierre wasn't taking the chance of leaving any trace behind. With one last check of Melinda's apartment, he headed back to theirs.

Chapter Ten

Melinda glared at Louis through eyes puffy and red from crying as he blocked her from leaving. The sight of him, sleep tousled and naked from the waist up, a dark brush of hair trailing down washboard abs disappearing as a thin line beneath low slung gray sweats, almost derailed her line of thinking. He didn't understand. She had to get back to her apartment. Make sure the bullets *had* destroyed her hard drives. And check on Manchu. Her poor baby was probably frightened out of his mind. Then... She blocked the image of the man on the floor, the blood, that threatened to overwhelm her. She didn't know what she was going to do.

Louis shook his head at her, his easygoing smile gone, his lips pressed together in a determined line. "You can't go back in there, *mon amour*. It's not safe."

"I have to go back in. I have to..."

Pierre entered the room, also naked from the waist up. Also wearing gray sweats that left little to the imagination. And she could imagine a lot. Especially knowing he was, without a doubt, going commando.

In one hand, he had two shopping bags and her backpack. In the other, her cat carrier, with a hissing and snarling Manchu inside.

Melinda dropped her laptop on the table and crouched in front of the cat carrier. "Manchu."

Amber eyes fixed on her for a second, then he hissed and spun away.

"Melinda, I've made sure your hard drives aren't salvageable." Pierre turned to his twin. "I wiped down your prints, Louis, but we can't stay here." His dark gaze swung her way, no less resolute than Louis'. "And neither can you, *mon amour*."

Pierre had checked on her hard drives? It confirmed what she already knew. There was only one reason someone would do that. Melinda rose from her knees, unwilling to be at a disadvantage. "You know I'm a hacker."

Louis and Pierre shared a look, some sort of silent communication passing between them.

Pierre set the cat carrier and the bags down. "We like to know who we share a building with. People in our line of business always do. It's a habit."

People in their line of business? Wolf Enterprises? "And what line of business would that be, exactly?"

Louis disappeared into his room, returned with his wallet and handed her a card, white with an image of a howling black wolf's head and the words Wolf Enterprises in elaborate silver beneath it. It didn't escape her notice the design on the card looked an awful lot like the silver motif on their leather wrist cuffs.

Her hands shook as she turned it over. Because of the last half hour's events, or because she feared what she would find? Maybe both.

The back was blank. No website, no phone number, no email, not even a bricks-and-mortar address.

Louis stood there, hands on his hips, watching her. "We're in security. Technical division. Computer experts."

Technical division. Computer experts. Of course they were. It all made sense now. Why she'd found so little on them. Why they hid their tech when they had guests over. Their awareness of the cameras. The twins were hackers. Like her, only they worked for a corporation. A highly secretive, exclusive one by the looks of the card. "Why are you in London?"

Louis shrugged, drawing her gaze to the play of muscles across his chest. "We had a job to do."

"There's nothing more we can tell you, Melinda," said Pierre. "Client confidentiality."

Melinda could understand that. They couldn't tell her any more than she could divulge information about her client, MysticMage. Or any of her clients. But their vague answer had her on edge. Or was that because barely fifteen minutes ago, someone had tried to kill her? And now there was a dead man in her flat.

She couldn't say she was sorry about that. Better him than her, but that didn't change the fact Louis had just killed a man. How could they be so calm after what had happened tonight? What the hell sort of security work were they involved in?

Her body shook, her knees weakening. Had Louis and Pierre not burst in, that shot would have found its mark and she'd be little more than a police report filed in the morning. If she stayed in her flat, she'd be in a police report for an entirely different reason. She slumped down on the sofa, her head in her hands. What the hell was she supposed to do?

The sofa dipped, and a muscled arm pulled her close. "Melinda. You're not alone. We can help you."

Pierre.

She shook her head. She couldn't involve them. That wasn't right. Not if she did what her heart was telling her she should do. Find MysticMage. She needed to make sure the woman was safe. Melinda's mother had never left her father, but she'd heard all the threats of what he would do if she ever tried to. She couldn't, wouldn't, allow any more violence to happen on her watch. Not because of her.

Pierre grasped her about the waist, and suddenly she was sitting not on the sofa, but on his lap, engulfed in his warmth, surrounded by his scent. Was it wrong if she took comfort from it? If only for a minute?

Louis dropped to his knees in front of her. Now they surrounded her, blocking out the world, and she longed to give into it. To stay here forever.

Louis cupped her face. "We can help you, Melinda. We have resources far beyond your imagination."

"Can you get me to San Francisco?" Her sarcasm hung in the air.

A shrug of shoulders from behind her. "*Oui*. You want to go to San Francisco? We can get you there."

Seriously?

For the second time in the last twenty-four hours, Melinda extricated herself from their embrace. "Thanks, but… This is not your concern. I've involved you enough already."

Louis got to his feet and laid a hand on her shoulder. "Please, Melinda. Someone tried to kill you tonight."

The concern in his hazel eyes was touching. She tucked her laptop into one shopping bag, threading her hand through both bags' straps and her backpack, and grabbed the cat carrier. "I'll be fine."

Would she? In all her years creating new identities for people, some very unsavory, she'd never encountered this situation. She guessed it'd only been a matter of time.

Pierre unfolded himself from the sofa. "How are you going to get out of the country?"

She pinched her brows together.

"Whoever sent that man to your apartment to kill you tracked you somehow. The moment you book a flight, the moment you hand over your passport at the airport…" Pierre rubbed his chin. "Who knows what they're capable of, what connections they have."

He had a point. She could hunker down somewhere in a seedy motel under a fake name until she could organize a new identity and passport, but that could take weeks. Did she have that sort of time? Not if she wanted to save her client from the same fate that had nearly been hers.

"And what are you going to do with your cat?" asked Louis. "Leave him at a shelter? You'll never get him through customs."

As though Manchu knew he was being discussed, he let out a plaintive meow. How could she leave him behind? Through some of her darkest days, he'd been her only friend.

Pierre crossed his arms over his gloriously naked chest. "We can."

The question in her eyes must have been obvious.

"Wolf Enterprises has a private jet." Pierre's lip quirked up. "And our brother lives in San Francisco.

He'll have a place where we can lie low while you do what you need to do."

It was tempting, but... "You can't just go gallivanting halfway across the world on a whim. Don't you have work to do?"

Pierre shrugged. "Nothing that won't improve with a bit of patience and time. Besides, I wouldn't mind catching up with our brother Gabriel. We haven't seen him since before Christmas. What do you think, Louis?"

Louis gently pulled the bags from her grasp, setting them on the coffee table. "I'd like to see our brother, too."

Pierre nodded. "It's settled, then. We're going to California."

Melinda gaped. They weren't serious? They barely knew her. She barely knew *them.*

"Louis, grab our stuff."

Pierre got on the phone, speaking in rapid French Melinda had no hope of understanding. By the time he ended the brief call, Louis was back, now wearing a shirt, with two overnight bags and two laptop bags.

Where the hell did they hide those when I went looking for them?

Pierre caught the shirt Louis flung in his direction and slipped it on. It boggled Melinda's mind she had room in her head to be disappointed they'd covered up.

Pierre hooked his hands through her bags and took the cat carrier, and a hissing Manchu. Numb, and a little bewildered, Melinda allowed the twins to lead her from their flat. She was doing this. Getting on a plane, a private jet, with two men she'd met only a few weeks ago. Flying to another country. She must be mad. If she wanted to get to MysticMage before her husband did,

Melinda didn't see she had a lot of choice. Pierre and Louis had saved her. That had to count for something.

It wasn't until she was safe in an Uber, sandwiched between the twins, her head resting back against the seat, did the vision of her attack and rescue come back to her. Not the dark shape of the intruder, or the flash of the red laser beam of his gun. No. The man, the twin, Louis, with half his body, the top half, contorted, shifting, changing as he tore the throat out of her attacker with his *bare teeth*.

Perhaps it was stress, the adrenaline of the moment, but Melinda could have sworn, in the shadowy darkness of her office, Louis had partly transformed into a wolf.

Chapter Eleven

Pierre had spent most of the drive to Biggin Hill Airport on the phone, organizing the pack's private jet, filing flight plans and smoothing their exit from London and entry into the United States. The cat wasn't a problem, despite what Louis had told Melinda. There were no quarantine restrictions for it. Organizing an immediate visa for him and Louis to travel to the United States posed some difficulty, but they had contacts. Melinda was an altogether different matter.

Laurent had updated them on the situation back at the apartment building. There would be an All-Points Bulletin out for Melinda now that the police were involved. Even if they could convince their contact to risk issuing her a visa, they still had to get her through customs. He'd called Gabriel again. His brother, through his mate Annabelle's coven, had put out the request. He didn't know what his brother had had to agree to, to get them what they needed — he could only hope Maxime wouldn't have his balls for it — but they'd found a shifter from another pack working at Buchanan Airfield willing to look the other way when they passed through customs. They were on their way to San Francisco. To find Cordelia.

Melinda, the cat carrier on the seat beside her — the feisty ball of ginger fur inside it calmer but wary — leaned her head against the window of the jet, her eyes closed and her laptop clutched to her chest like it was her only lifeline. There was so much they were keeping from her — their true identity, their true purpose in coming to London, the reasons they were so willing to help her. Both reasons. Finding out she was the mate of not one, but two werewolves would be a shock. Learning they'd used malware to track her down and were intent on apprehending her client, ridding the pack and the world of a malevolent threat...

The concern in Louis' eyes could only mirror his own. Somehow, they had to get Melinda to see Cordelia for who she was, before she uncovered their deception. They had eight, nearly nine hours to come up with a solution.

Louis unclipped his safety belt. "She's exhausted. She needs to rest. In comfort." He plucked her laptop from her arms and set it aside then unbuckled her belt and lifted her in his arms.

She grumbled a little, snuggling against Louis' chest. Pierre eyed the laptop. Now was their chance. Instead, he followed Louis to the back of the jet, to the private bedroom. He pulled back the covers on the bed and Louis laid her down on the cool sheets, slipping her shoes off.

Louis put her glasses on the small side table. "Should we...?" Louis whispered, gesturing at her clothes. "Denim isn't exactly comfortable to sleep in."

He'd love nothing more than to see their little mate naked but for her undergarments, but would Melinda be upset when she awoke? He nodded, the comfort of their mate winning out. Add it to the list of their transgressions. Between the two of them, they gently maneuvered her out of her jeans and sweater.

He sucked in a breath. *Putain*, she was beautiful. White lace cupped her perfect small breasts. More lace slipped between her slender thighs, stark against the warmth of her golden skin. Her silky hair splayed across the pillow and her dark lashes fluttered against her cheek.

Louis sat on the bed beside her and brushed her hair from her forehead. "Makes you want to crawl into bed with her, doesn't it?"

A rumble rose in his chest. *Oui*, it did, but he stepped back. Melinda stirred and sleep-glazed eyes stared up at them. Confusion fluttered across her face, her hands skimming over her bare stomach.

"Just wanted you to be comfortable, *mon amour*. We didn't peek." Louis backed away. "Much."

Melinda's arm snaked out and grabbed his. "Please don't go." Dark eyes implored them. "I don't want to be alone."

He shared a glance with Louis, nodded, and his brother sank back onto the bed, wrapping her in his arms and resting her head on his shoulder. But their little mate wasn't content with the simple comfort his brother offered. She pressed her body flush against Louis, rubbing herself all over him. Pierre's nostrils flared and his cock did a stellar impression of a flagpole. Louis' eyes rolled back in his head, and Pierre imagined his twin to be similarly struggling in his sweats as he was.

She snuggled into Louis, her hands fluttering over his chest and neck. "I can still see him, standing there with his gun." She dropped little urgent kisses against the column of Louis' throat. "I don't want to see him anymore."

Louis peeled her away from him, the strain of not pouncing on her, not taking her up on what she was clearly offering, writ in the tautness of his lips and the clenching of his jaw.

"Make me forget." Her brown gaze flicked between the two of them. "Please."

"Louis." Pierre shook his head, cautioning Louis against action. It was going to kill him not to give her what she wanted, too, but now was not the time. Not when fear, shock and stress were leading her actions. Not when she might come to regret her decision. They had enough challenges ahead of them where she was concerned, without racking up more.

Louis glared at him and held his ground. His twin was not one for patience, nor restraint, but he rarely went against Pierre. Not when it mattered. And it mattered now, more than it ever had.

Melinda ground her hips against Louis' groin, and latched onto his throat, sucking down hard. His brother moaned and cupped the back of her head, holding her in place. He rolled his hips against hers and their little mate shivered.

"You're wrong, Pierre. She wants this. She *needs* this."

Melinda pushed Louis back onto the bed and straddled him, lifting her arms above her head and arching her spine. *Putain.*

Louis groaned, clenching his hands around her thighs and holding her in place as he rolled his hips, grinding against her.

"Yes, Louis. Yes."

Her words were a mere whisper, full of need, and if it were possible, they would have made his cock harder.

"I'll give you what you need, *mon amour*. Fuck Pierre. He can watch if he doesn't want to join in."

Melinda gasped and her spine arched more. She liked the idea of him watching Louis fuck her. *He* liked the idea of watching Louis fuck her.

He gripped his cock through the soft material of his sweatpants. "Give her what she wants, Louis." His voice was rough even to his own ears. "Give her what we *all* need."

Would she come to regret this? Maybe. Did she care right now? Not one iota. Melinda rubbed her core against Louis' thick length, biting back the moan threatening to spill from her mouth. Since she'd fled their flat, the bedroom, Pierre's bed, her body had been primed for this. Wanted this. The subsequent events of the night, her near death experience, had done little to dampen her desire. She needed to be close to someone, to wipe away her fear of what had transpired, and what was yet to come. For a while, to lose herself in something so overwhelming her mind would quiet and her heart would race for an altogether different reason. Louis could give her that. Louis *and* Pierre.

Melinda half turned. Pierre leaned against the wall, one hand disappearing beneath the band of his gray sweats, his beautiful hazel eyes fixed on her. She clenched her thighs around Louis' hips.

Louis sat up and wrapped his arms around her, pulling her tight against him. "Pierre likes to watch, almost as much as he likes to fuck," he whispered, his breath hot across her cheek.

He took her mouth in his, gentle, teasing, tugging on her bottom lip. "Let's give him a show he'll never forget."

Her body sizzled, and she glanced at Pierre again from beneath hooded lids. Have sex while he watched? A shiver ran up her spine. Something inside her, careless and a little wild, pushed to the surface by the knowledge she was alive, and had things gone differently she might not have been, broke free.

She rocked her hips again, riding Louis' hard length, never taking her eyes from Pierre. *Yes.*

A deep growl started up in Pierre's throat, more animal than human, and a musky scent filled the room.

"Shall we give him a show? Do you like the sound of that, *bébé*?" Louis nibbled down the side of her throat. "Pierre does. I do, too."

His hands were rubbing circles all over her back as his lips worked along her collarbone. He flicked the clasp of her bra open and slipped the straps from her shoulders. The fabric of his shirt teased her already peaked nipples. Still she couldn't look away from Pierre. In the periphery of her vision, his hand moved up and down his hidden length, slow strokes, keeping in time with the lazy roll of Louis' hips pressing his cock against her clit.

Then she was being lifted, turned around and sat back down on Louis' lap. She faced Pierre, and he watched on as Louis cupped her breasts, rolling her nipples between his fingers. Pierre's nostrils flared, a low groan slipping out between his bared teeth. To be the center of such desire, such blatant need, was intoxicating. Melinda reveled in it, arching her back, thrusting her swollen nipples at him, all but begging Louis for more.

As though he heard her silent pleas, he gave her more, sucking along the cord of her neck, and sliding his hand lower, leaving goosebumps and trembles in his wake as he traversed her stomach. Lower still, he slipped his hand beneath the lace of her panties and found her clit. She threw her head back and let out a moan so full of hunger she could barely fathom it had come from her mouth.

"Look at how she bares her neck for us. *Putain,* Pierre. *J'ai veux la mordre. De la revendiquer.* Here. Now."

What had he said? What did he want to do, here and now? Please let it be what she hoped. Louis' fingers circled her clit. She teetered on the edge.

"No." The single word cracked across the room.

Louis growled, and his finger stopped circling. *No.* She'd be a mess if he left her unsatisfied. Again. She couldn't face it twice in one night. Not after —

"Soon," promised Pierre. "Now stop messing around and give me that show you promised me. I'm not going to last much longer."

Yes.

Louis chuckled against her neck. "*Oui*, Pierre."

His finger resumed its slow circling, and Melinda shuddered her relief, chasing it, wanting more.

"*Putain*, Pierre. She's so wet. I can't wait to be inside her."

Melinda mewled. *That's what I want. Louis inside me.*

He slipped his fingers in, first one, then a second. She gasped and squeezed her eyes shut. *So good.* The rub of his thumb on her clit worked in tandem with the thrust of his fingers, wet sucking sounds mingling with her harsh pants.

"Look at Pierre, *bébé*. Let him see it all."

Her eyelids fluttered, but she was too lost in the delicious slide of Louis' thick fingers against her G-spot, the pressure building in her core and the base of her spine. She was close. Oh, so close.

"Open your eyes, Melinda. Look at me."

The punch of command in Pierre's voice had her snapping her eyes open and giving him what he wanted. Those beautiful eyes full of hunger, for her, they captured her, and held her prisoner. Dark shadows swirled in their depths, mesmerizing her, dragging her deeper until she thought she might drown in them and be lost forever.

Her release hit her faster than a bullet train. She clamped down on Louis' fingers, threw her head back and opened her mouth on a silent scream, her body shuddering through the best orgasm she'd had in...in forever.

She collapsed into a spineless heap, her chest heaving. Louis slipped his fingers free and gathered her close.

"Beautiful," he murmured, turning her face to kiss her lips, gentle, reverent, as though she were the most precious thing in his world.

Then Pierre was there, cupping her face and taking her mouth in his, taking her deep. Soul deep. She clutched at them both, afraid to let them go. Afraid this moment might end.

Pierre pulled away with a final suck of her bottom lip. "*Oui*. Beautiful. And all ours."

Yes, she wanted to be theirs. Here. Now. Between the two of them. Wanted them both in a way that would stay with her, forever imprinted in her memory. Something to warm her. To fantasize over when they were gone, and she was alone again with nothing but her screens, her cat and her work. Something that would ease the emptiness of battery-powered relief. A moment in time where she'd been truly alive.

"Playtime is over," growled Pierre.

Disappointment burned in her chest. Then Pierre kicked off his shoes, ripped his shirt over his head and dropped his sweatpants.

He stood gloriously naked, his cock jutting out, slick with pre-cum. "Now we fuck."

Louis tipped her onto the bed. "You thought we were done, *bébé*?" He chuckled. "Oh, Melinda. We've only just started."

Chapter Twelve

It was over an eight-hour flight to San Francisco, and Louis planned to spend as much of that as he could giving their little mate all the pleasure she could take. He suspected, in her current state of mind, she could take a lot. He was going to make sure, when this night was over, they would've imprinted themselves on her so thoroughly Melinda wouldn't want to, wouldn't be able to walk away from them. Ever.

The road ahead of them would be a rocky one. They were werewolves. She was human. But that was a hurdle many Langeais wolves would face. It would've been easier had she, like Gabriel's mate, Annabelle, known they were shifters. It wasn't to be, and Louis wouldn't change their mate. Not for anything. She was perfect. Except for one little detail. She worked for the enemy.

Unknowingly, but that didn't change the fact Cordelia, the witch with a vendetta against the

Langeais wolves, was her client. And it was their job to track Cordelia down.

Pierre kneeled on the bed in front of her, and Louis thrust thoughts of the witch out of his mind. Tonight was all about Melinda.

With her attention focused on Pierre, he brought his wolf forward enough to extend a claw on each hand, but nothing more. Until she had accepted they were in her life permanently, they couldn't afford to reveal who — what — they were. Right now, she saw them as a means to an end. An enjoyable way to relieve the stress and the horror of the night. She was going to be in for a surprise, *non*?

He snagged the white lace band of her panties on either side and ripped through them. She gasped as they dropped.

He gave her a slap on her bare ass. "On your hands and knees, *bébé*."

She squealed, but jumped to obey.

Merde. A prettier sight he had never seen. Melinda presenting, her pink pussy all wet and glistening. His loose sweats were too constricting. He was wearing too many fucking clothes. Time to rectify that. He slipped off the bed, toed off his shoes and shucked his shirt and sweatpants, his cock springing free, eager and ready. It had been in this perpetual state since the moment he'd stood outside her door, inviting her to their apartment to taste his nuts.

His nostrils flared at the thought of her mouth on him doing exactly that. Tasting his nuts. Pierre gripped a hand in Melinda's hair, lifting her head level with his groin. She licked her lips. Lucky Pierre. But he wouldn't be left wanting. Not at all.

He grasped Melinda by her hips and ran his tongue along her glistening slit. She moaned, and all but shoved her pussy into his face. He chuckled against her lips and her whole body jerked.

"Does she taste good, Louis?"

He gave her another lick. "Mm. *Paradis.*"

Then he set to laving her with his tongue, holding her wiggling ass tight, keeping her still, bringing her to the brink, then switching up the rhythm until she was quivering all over.

Pierre growled and fisted his cock in his hand. She reached for him, placing her hand over his, nearly losing her balancing and toppling over.

Louis abandoned his feasting and grabbed her waist with both hands, keeping her steady.

"No, don't stop," she pleaded. "I need —"

Pierre filled her mouth with the bulbous head of his cock, silencing her demands. His twin's eyes rolled back in his head and his chest heaved. A hand still gripped in her hair, Pierre guided her up and down his length. A musky scent filled the room, and a muscle ticked in Pierre's jaw. His brother's vaunted control was close to breaking. Fuck, Louis wanted in on that. Wanted to feel it, too.

Holding her steady with one hand, he tapped her inner thighs, forcing her to part them. On his knees, he positioned himself between them, his cock rejoicing as it made contact with her wet heat. She pushed back against him, moaning, her mouth full of Pierre. Slick and coating him in her juices with every thrust between her lips, it took everything Louis had not to embarrass himself. To not finish before they'd even started. Pierre always railed at him for being impulsive, impatient. His twin would never let him live it down if he did.

Melinda jerked away from Pierre. "Condoms?"

Putain. They didn't need condoms. As werewolves, they were immune to disease. As Langeais wolves, they couldn't impregnate a human. But Melinda didn't know that, and he couldn't tell her. Pierre disappeared, and when he returned, he threw a small square packet at him.

Merde. He didn't want to wear one. Wanted nothing between him and his little mate. Melinda squirmed, concern lacing her scent.

He tore the packet open with his teeth and slipped the latex over his length. For Melinda, he'd wear it.

Louis eased back, lined himself up with her entrance and thrust.

Putain. I'm inside her. My mate. Our mate.

Louis was no saint. Neither was Pierre. They'd had many a woman in their beds, alone and together. Werewolves were highly sexual beings. Yet nothing he had ever experienced before, no woman he had ever fucked before, could compare to this. This woman. No, *their* woman, taking him deep, her channel fluttering around him, squeezing him tight. Their little *chouquette* who had pulled them into her world with her skills and intrigued them with the cause she championed. He'd brave a million old lady apartments and floral duvets again to be here right now.

Louis planned to do this many times over in his long life, from now on with Melinda and only Melinda, but nothing would beat this first time, seating himself balls deep inside her. He'd remember this moment forever.

Louis moaned. "She feels so good, Pierre."

"*Oui.*" His brother's voice held an awe he'd never heard from him before. He was feeling it, too.

Melinda gave an impatient wiggle of her ass, and he chuckled. "*Oui, chouquette.* I will give you what you're wanting." He rolled his hips, pressing deeper, and she moaned her pleasure around Pierre's cock.

"Stop playing, Louis." There was a snap of command in Pierre's voice. "I'm not going to last much longer."

Who's the impatient one now? But Louis, sensation sizzling in the base of his spine, heeded his brother's words. Gripping her hips to keep her steady, he thrust into her faster and faster, setting a furious rhythm matched only by Pierre. Melinda grasped hold of Pierre's thighs, steadying herself as they rocked back and forward on the bed, the drone of the jet's engines no match for the symphony of their mate's moans and mewls of pleasure. Louis could listen to those gorgeous sounds on replay and never tire of them.

"I'm going to come."

At Pierre's hoarse shout, Melinda's pussy clamped down on Louis' cock and his release ripped through him. He stiffened, resisting the howl that rose in his throat, his canines punching through his gums, and Louis could have sworn his brain, his life essence, his soul were exiting his body through his dick and pouring into Melinda. He couldn't stop coming.

Louis collapsed in a sweaty mess, taking a shuddering Melinda with him. Pierre stood at the end of the bed, wrecked, his chest heaving and a look of shocked awe on his face. Louis chuckled and buried his face in Melinda's hair, scenting her. She smelled of them now. Satisfaction burned in Pierre's eyes. *Oui*, Louis liked it, too.

Pierre ducked out of the room and returned with a damp cloth. Melinda stirred as he started wiping her face, her chin, cleaning her up.

Melinda struggled to sit up. "I can do that." She grabbed for the washcloth.

Pierre held the cloth out of her reach.

"Shh. Let him do it, *chouquette.*" Louis held her firm in his arms. "Let him take care of you. It's what he likes to do. He'll be a grumpy…bear all day if he can't."

Merde. He'd almost slipped and said wolf. Pierre glared at him. His brother had caught his hesitation. Had she?

After a moment's pause, she relaxed into his arms and let Pierre wipe her down, dragging the cloth over her pert little breasts, cleaning up the evidence of his release. With a refresh of the cloth, Pierre continued his thorough ministrations between her thighs. She lay there in his arms, limp and satiated, and it wasn't long before she slipped into a deep and, he hoped, dreamless sleep.

Pierre tossed the cloth and returned to the bed, and they cocooned her between them. Nothing in this world was more precious. They would keep her safe. Louis would give his life for her without a second thought. Pierre, too. The question was — would she let them?

Pierre slipped on his sweats. Melinda still slept, wrapped in Louis' arms, one leg hooked over his twin's thigh. He wanted to stay with them, maybe go another round with their hot little mate, have her wake up with both of them beside her, but… Louis met his gaze, and his brother nodded. He understood. In the main cabin, unattended, was Melinda's laptop.

It pained him to deceive her like this, but there was a lot at stake, and that laptop was the key. Finding Cordelia before Melinda did was the best outcome. For the pack and for their mate. He didn't want that ruthless old witch anywhere near her. All he could hope was Melinda would see the end result justified the means. If it didn't... There wasn't enough cognac in the world to drown out that sorrow. Maxime could attest to that.

He'd need time to crack Melinda's encryption. With any luck, she would sleep for a few hours. At least one of them would be with her when she woke up. He couldn't bear her thinking it'd only been sex to them. A frightened woman in need of solace, an opportunity, and nothing more.

With his own laptop open in front of him, he booted up Melinda's. This wouldn't be easy. In the three months since Christmas, Melinda had proved herself to be a worthy adversary. It'd been no simple matter to track her down, despite having the neat piece of code he and Louis had created. A warmth settled in his chest. He liked that their mate was like them. A hacker. He liked it more that she used her skills to help those in need. But her apartment, while not high-end, didn't come cheap, and righteous crusades didn't pay well. That had left her exposed to people like Cordelia.

Melinda's screen saver popped up. Time to get to work.

Chapter Thirteen

It took Melinda a moment to recognize where she was. On a private jet, bound for San Francisco. With two drop-dead gorgeous twins. One of whose bare chest she still had her face smooshed up against. Another moment to collect herself and remember what had happened, what she'd done — what *they'd* done, *all three of them* — before she'd fallen asleep.

Oh hell. She'd pleaded for it. For sex. On her hands and knees, let Louis take her from behind, as she took Pierre...

She clamped her thighs at the memory.

"You're awake, *chouquette.*"

She raised her head to a blur of dark hair and white teeth. "Louis? Pierre?"

She scrambled around, searching for her glasses. With gentle hands, he slid them on her face. Hazel eyes and a cheeky grin greeted her. Louis. Despite his smile, there was something mournful in his eyes, a dance of dark shadows within his irises. It made her long to reach out and touch him, comfort him. Stupid idea.

She pushed at his chest and he released her, and she rolled away from him, dragging the sheet with her to hide her nakedness. He let her take it without comment, but it left him lying there in all his bare glory. Heat rose up her neck and face. She should have kept her glasses off.

Melinda turned her back on Louis, snatched her clothes from the floor, left Louis sprawled on the bed and shut herself in the cramped toilet cubicle. Flipping the toilet lid down, she sat, her head in hands, letting her clothes fall to the floor. Through the gap in her fingers, she spied her ruined knickers. She held them up. The waistband was torn in two places. Useless, except to remind her that in a moment of weakness, she'd sought comfort in their arms. They'd been happy to oblige. Two men in her bed. *At the same time.*

She glanced at her reflection in the mirror and wished she hadn't. Staring back at her were her mother's eyes. It reminded her of why she was here. Of the woman — the eighty-something-year-old woman — whose life was in danger. And while she couldn't do a lot from forty-five-thousand feet in the air, she couldn't afford to waste time dwelling on what was a one-time thing. The twins wouldn't make a big deal of it. She suspected they'd been here before. Why should she react any differently?

Avoiding the mirror, she dressed minus her knickers, washed her face and combed her fingers through her hair. When she stepped out of the cubicle and into the main cabin, bright daylight streamed through the jet's windows. She'd been too tired, too emotionally drained to take it all in last night, but now, in the clear light of the morning, what she'd begun to suspect was abundantly clear. Wolf Enterprises, the twins, had money. Serious money.

This wasn't your standard private jet. This was top of the line, no expense spared luxury. From the leather armchairs to the black-accented paneling. The plush carpet beneath her shoes and the galley with crystal glassware and bottles of top-end liquor. That it had a private bedroom suite should have clued her in.

There was no sign of Louis, but Pierre sat at the front of the plane with his back to her, tapping away on a laptop. She ignored the little flutter in her stomach at the sight of his bare torso.

"Morning, Melinda."

He didn't lift his head from his work, and it gave her a brief reprieve. A moment to get her wayward libido under control.

"Morning," she said, walking down the aisle toward him.

He looked up, concern in his eyes. "Did you sleep all right, *chouquette*?"

There was that word again. "*Chouquette*?"

"Mm. Louis' choice." A bemused smile played across his lips. "It is more common to say *mon chou*, but—"

"*Chouquettes* are my favorite pastry," said Louis, striding out of the bedroom, black jeans slung low on his hips, his chest bare. "Small, but sweet and oh, so tasty. Like you."

Melinda ducked her head. In the bright light of day, one half naked man was enough. Two, almost more than she could bear. It made her long for a repeat of last night.

Louis held out her overnight bag. "I thought you might like a fresh change of clothes." He smirked. "And a new pair of panties."

"Stop teasing her, Louis. She's had a rough night, not least because the two of us pounced on her."

Nice of him to lay the blame on themselves. She knew — they all did — that wasn't what had happened.

Melinda grabbed her bag from Louis and pushed past him. With these two around, knickers were a must. At the bedroom door she turned, the twins hunched over, deep in quiet conversation. About her? Or about the job they were leaving behind in London? She'd like to know what that was. What type of security Wolf Enterprises undertook. Celebrities? Government officials? Or did they stray into the darker side of society? Clients like those *she* found on the dark web?

She ducked into the bedroom and changed, ignoring a set of red lacy underwear Pierre had packed in favor of a white cotton bra and panties. Much more together once she was no longer going commando, she returned to the main cabin. Louis was gone, leaving her alone with Pierre.

Melinda fussed over Manchu, giving him a cuddle, water and some cat biscuits before taking a seat opposite Pierre. In front of him sat his laptop. To the side, pushed up against the wall of the jet, hers. Had he...? Suspicion curled in her gut. What if...? What if she'd made a terrible mistake? Trusting them? They'd said they were taking her to California. How would she know any different if they weren't?

She swiveled in her seat, staring down the aisle toward the front of the plane. "Has Louis gone to talk to the pilot?"

"*Oui.* He's checking that everything is fine with the flight plans we filed. That Buchanan Airfield is expecting us, and our contact is in place to make sure we get through customs smoothly."

Oh. Buchanan Airfield. It sounded American. She reached for her laptop. "Does the jet have Wi-Fi?" She'd do a search, though there was nothing to stop Pierre from lying to her.

He cocked an eyebrow at her over his screen. "Of course it does. We're hackers. What use would a jet be if we didn't?"

Yeah. Stupid question. If she had a private jet, she'd make sure she had connectivity, too.

"Melinda, about last night…"

She shook her head. "I don't want to talk about it. What happened between us was a one — "

"I meant in your apartment."

Oh. She blinked. Well, that told her where she stood. Already forgotten.

He tapped a few keys on his laptop and swiveled it around to face her. On the screen, a photo of a man's neck with a tattoo of an elaborate F. "Have you ever seen this tattoo before?"

It was pretty. The font stylized, interconnecting swirls curling around it, and two crossed swords suspended above it. She shook her head. "No. Why?"

"The man who attacked you had one."

A chill ran down her spine. They'd taken a photo of it? Or had they hacked into the police database? But where was the blood? There would have had to have been blood. Louis had… What? Ripped the man's throat out with his bare teeth? Had she imagined that part? Fabricated a kind of horror flick version of events as a way of dealing with what had happened? It was all a blur, compounded by the darkness. Her cowering in the closet, the wail of the alarm, the intruder standing over her holding a gun.

Louis returned to the cabin and threw himself into a chair next to Manchu. Her cat hissed. Like Melinda, the events in her flat were still too fresh in his mind. Louis grinned at her, and she tried to imagine those perfect white teeth being capable of ripping apart a man's throat.

She raked her hands through her hair. These men didn't deserve her suspicion. Without them, she'd be dead. "I never said thank you for last night. In my flat. For being there. For stopping... Thank you." She swept her gaze over the cabin. "And for flying me all the way to California. In your company's private jet, no less. You must have a very understanding boss."

Leather squeaked as Pierre leaned back in his chair. "We wouldn't have had it any other way."

Louis nodded, backing up his brother's statement.

Melinda didn't know what to make of the emotion that fluttered in her chest, so she ignored it and booted up her laptop. The low battery warning lit up her screen. Odd. Her battery had been full when the intruder had interrupted her, and though she'd just closed the lid, sending it into sleep mode, it shouldn't have drained the battery completely. Had Pierre been messing with her computer? While she slept in his brother's arms? The thought stung.

If he had, it wouldn't take much for her to find out. But would she be happy with the answer? Despite Pierre's brush off about their tango between the sheets, she really wanted them to be the good guys.

Chapter Fourteen

Pierre caught the narrowing of Melinda's eyes from behind dark frames as she plugged her laptop in. Did she suspect? Did she know? Had he tripped another of her trigger alarms? She was good at that. Hiding IDS alerts in her work. If he'd found her password, if he'd logged on, he would have destroyed any evidence he'd been there, but he hadn't got that far.

Though he knew as much as anyone about Melinda as could be gleaned from her digital footprint, and from watching her for three weeks, he'd not bothered to try cracking her encryption on his own. No, Melinda was good a hacker. She would have a strong password, void of anything personal. So he'd connected his laptop with hers, and set running a clever program Louis had developed for instances such as this.

As it churned away, he'd sent a neat little virus to the server hosting the security feed for their apartment. Any evidence, any footage of either his or Louis' presence there, gone with the press of a key. He'd corrupted the entire security system, and anything else using that server. Then he'd wiped any stored footage in the cameras. The ones in Melinda's apartment, too.

He'd searched the police database for early reports on the callout to her apartment. A call from Laurent earlier had let them know he'd taken care of the Faucherian. How he'd managed that when the police had already been on the scene, he hadn't asked. All that mattered was the body was unlikely to ever see the light of day again. But that wasn't their only problem. The crime scene techs had gathered and bagged a lot of evidence before Laurent had arrived. Taking and disposing of the body was the best he could manage. The rest was up to them.

Pierre needed to know what evidence the police had collected and logged. If there was anything significant, or that implicated either him or Louis. If there was any way he could keep Melinda's name out of it, and stop the police from following her here. That her passport was in her name and her apartment bought under a false identity with no easy-to-find links to her was helpful.

He'd made headway on her laptop encryption, his program crunching its way through a trillion possible password combinations as he'd worked, when his acute hearing had picked up the sounds of stirring in the bedroom. He'd cursed, removed the connection between her laptop and his, shoved it aside, and closed all the tabs he'd had open relating to Melinda as she'd stepped out. But their mate was clever. Observant.

Pierre held his breath while Melinda tapped away at her keyboard. What she found seemed to satisfy her, the lines on her forehead smoothing out and the acrid scent of suspicion in the air dissipating.

He released his breath in silent relief. *Thank fuck.*

"Talk to us, Melinda," he said. "Give us something to work with so we know what we're up against here."

With each lie they told, whether direct or of omission, they dug themselves in a deeper hole they may never climb out of.

Louis leaned forward, his elbows on his knees. "*Chouquette*, we can't help you if you don't tell us what's going on."

It hardly seemed fair, the two of them against her. Pierre reached across the table and linked his fingers through hers. "I understand your need to protect your client's privacy, but is there anything you *can* tell us that might help us know what to expect?"

She looked at him then, over her glasses. He hadn't known he had a thing for glasses, but on Melinda they were as sexy as fuck.

Melinda puffed out a breath and pushed her frames back up her nose. "I create new identities for people, okay? One of my clients..." She shook her head. "I have clients I do work for from a women's refuge, helping them hide from their abusive husbands. It's something I do because..." A haunted look flashed across her face. "Because I can. I have *other* clients who pay a lot of money for my skills."

"There's a lot of reasons people need a new identity," said Louis. "Many of them not good."

"Of course, but this one—and believe me, she's paying like all the rest of them—she's more like the women I help from the refuge."

Cordelia? A battered wife? Non, non, non. Never. "Are you sure?"

"I've been doing this for a lot of years, so yeah, I'm sure."

Pierre rubbed his hand across the stubble on his chin. Melinda thinking Cordelia was a victim wasn't good. Not for them, for any chance they had with their mate and not for Melinda.

"And her husband has a lot of money and resources. I've created six identities for her, coded with alarms should someone try to trace her through them. Five times someone's cracked them. Her husband has engaged his own hacker, and he's good." She flipped the lid down on her laptop. "The last time, the son of a bitch hit me with malware. That's how he found me, the guy with the tattoo, I guess."

Pierre didn't dare take his gaze off Melinda to look at his twin, but he didn't have to, to know his brother was experiencing the same conflicting emotions – guilt, and a sense of relief they may never have to tell Melinda what they'd done.

"I've already contacted my client, warning her I might have been compromised. I did it before I came to your apartment last night. There's been no response. I'm worried."

That explained Melinda's late-night visit from a Faucherian.

"Your client's in San Francisco, I take it," said Louis.

Pierre forced himself to lean back in his chair, as if they were discussing nothing more important than Louis' morning gateau selection. They couldn't appear to be too eager.

Melinda nodded. "Yes. I believe she is."

Pierre kept a lid on his jubilation. All this time Cordelia had been right under Gabriel's nose. Not in Russia, China, or Switzerland. She'd never left the United States. She'd never left the damn city. Gabriel and the coven had turned over every rock, used every spell and resource they had to find her. He and Louis had spent weeks trolling through every database they could think of, searching for any information that might lead to her whereabouts—tax records, land records, digitized records of old newspapers. They'd found nothing.

Then identities had started popping up in different countries. So many they'd suspected it was a way to hide her real movements, Cordelia fleeing to another country. A time-traveling witch could turn up anywhere and start a new life, but in the modern world she'd need identification. One of the many they'd found had to be the real one. But none of them were, because she *hadn't gone anywhere*. They were nothing but a distraction. He wanted to punch his fist through the jet's paneling. How could he and Louis have been so stupid?

But where in San Francisco was she hiding? They'd found her cabin in the woods. The one where Cordelia's henchmen had taken Annabelle when they'd kidnapped her. All the King family members and their homes had been under surveillance for months. The dilapidated apartment building in the Tenderloin district had yielded nothing but an abandoned luxury suite on the top floor. The two other properties, linked not to Cordelia, but to dummy corporations and fake charities, had also proved fruitless.

Where the fuck is she?

"That settles it then." He leaned forward and put his elbows on the table, keeping his expression neutral. "We go to San Francisco and rescue your client."

There would be no *rescuing*.

"No." Melinda's voice was sharp. "No," she said, softening her tone. "While I'm grateful for all your help, I won't compromise your safety any further. This is my problem, not yours."

Compromise their safety? They were werewolves, for fuck's sake. Melinda was but a fragile human. For now. But she didn't know any of that, and she had no clue how ruthless Cordelia was. Or the powers the woman had at her disposal. That she wasn't some beaten-down, terrified woman running from her husband in desperate need of salvation.

Like hell Melinda would go anywhere without them by her side. Not to the grocery store, a café and especially not after Cordelia. "What about your safety, Melinda? You can't help anybody if you're dead."

Melinda flinched. Harsh, but true, and it drove his point home.

Louis was out of his seat and kneeling before her. He cupped her face. "*Chouquette*, a man tried to shoot you last night."

Fear flickered in her eyes and tainted her scent, but the determined set of her jaw remained.

Pierre clasped both hands around hers. "This is the type of thing Wolf Enterprises does. What *we* do. Let us help you. Think of us as your personal bodyguards."

"*Oui*. Very sexy bodyguards, *non*?" teased Louis.

Melinda cracked a hesitant smile.

"Everyone will be jealous." Louis side-eyed him. "Mostly because of me. I'm the better-looking twin. Pierre's the oldest. That's how you tell us apart."

There were as many differences between them as there were similarities. Would she notice? With time, he hoped so.

Melinda's gaze bounced between the two of them. "Bodyguards?"

Pierre gave her hands another gentle squeeze. "*Oui*."

A relaxing of her shoulders, a brief nod and the unmistakable change in the air, from fear to relief. "Okay. But I pay you for your services."

Pierre snarled. *Fuck, no.*

"I pay you," she said, her voice firm. "That makes me your boss, and you have to back off when I tell you to."

This time it was Louis who snarled.

Chin jutted out, she stared them down. "It's this way or not at all. I pay you, or we part ways as soon as we're through customs in San Francisco."

"Fine," he growled. Let her think what she liked. He'd create a damn invoice for her if that's what made her happy, made her think she had some control, but she wouldn't be paying them a single euro. And he and Louis were never going to leave her side. No matter what.

Chapter Fifteen

They breezed through customs with little fanfare, except for Manchu's caterwauling and hissing when the customs officer peeked into his cat carrier. The twins flanked her, guiding her to a waiting car like she was some sort of celebrity or foreign dignitary. It was an unfamiliar sensation, someone looking out for her. She liked it, but she shouldn't get too used to it. It was temporary. And paid for.

The ride from the airport was uneventful, and they were soon pulling to a stop beneath the portico of a palatial building complete with Grecian columns. The Ritz-Carlton. *Nice.* As Pierre collected the key from the front desk, Melinda did a slow spin around the foyer — a picture of marble floors, chandeliers, and understated elegance.

In the lift, Pierre swiped the key card and pressed the button for their floor. *The penthouse suite?* She shouldn't be surprised. A private jet, the penthouse suite. Wolf Enterprises had deep pockets. She might come to regret insisting on paying the twins for their services. No. Whatever it cost, even if it ate up all her savings, she was on surer ground with things between them as business only. Money got results. Trust… It'd been a long time since she'd trusted anyone.

Then again, she'd got on a plane and flown to a different country – and had wild sex – with two men she barely knew. She could chalk that up to the stress of the moment. The shock of being confronted in her own flat by a man with a gun. The twins' take-charge attitude, and because they'd offered her the only plausible choice in the circumstances. She could only hope it didn't come back to bite her on the ass.

The lift swished open into a lobby, and once again, the twins flanked her as they crossed the vestibule and into the suite. Two people, framed by floor to ceiling windows overlooking the San Francisco skyline, rose from the leather sofa. A woman, lithe, tall and gorgeous. A Xena Warrior Princess. Or a Lady Sith. Beside her, Melinda would look like a pixie.

And a man, a big man. The family resemblance was obvious. This must be Pierre's and Louis' brother, Gabriel. He had the same dark hair curling at the nape of his neck, the same golden skin, the same smile. He was a little rougher, lacking the suaveness of Pierre, and more serious, Louis' cheerfulness absent. Where Pierre and Louis were tall and muscular, Gabriel was a mountain of a man.

If the twins were the technical support, Gabriel must be the muscle. Director of Operations. Chief of Security. He wore the same leather wrist cuff with the silver wolf motif as the twins. The woman, too. Because they were all part of the co-operative? Wolf Enterprises?

Gabriel grinned and enfolded Louis in a bear hug, then turned to Pierre, dragging him in and clapping him on the back. "Good to see you, brothers. When was it? Before Christmas when we talked, face to face?"

Gabriel looked past the twins, his gaze settling on her, scrutinizing her from head to toe. Had the twins told him why they were here? What had happened in her flat? Was he angry she'd dragged his brothers into her drama? She must have met his approval, for he nodded, a jerk of his chin.

"Gabe, Stef—" Pierre held his hand at the small of her back. "This is Melinda Cheng. Melinda, this is my brother, Gabriel, and Stefanie, another member of Wolf Enterprises and a close family friend."

Melinda set the cat carrier down. "Hi. Nice to meet you both."

Gabriel quirked an eyebrow at the carrier. "What is that?"

"Manchu, my cat."

Gabriel leaned closer. "A cat?"

Manchu opened one amber eye. He took one look at the big man and hissed and spat, arching his back, his fur standing on end. Then he started yowling.

Gabriel winced, holding a hand to his ear. "How is it possible something so small can make such a wretched noise?"

Melinda rushed over to the carrier. "I'm sorry. He's normally a really placid cat." What'd got into Manchu? She opened the cage and reached for him, but the ginger feline wasn't interested in being comforted. He tore past her and took off up the floating staircase.

"Oh. I'm *so* sorry. I'll just... I'll go catch him." Flustered, Melinda took off after him.

"Don't worry, Melinda," Louis called after her. "I think we can all cope with one little cat."

In a penthouse suite? She didn't think so. Gabriel wouldn't be too impressed if he clawed that expensive sofa.

She found Manchu hiding under the big king-sized bed in the main bedroom. She gave up cajoling and, risking being scratched and bitten, grabbed him by the scruff of the neck and dragged the terrified kitty into her arms. He clung to her, nails sharp against her skin through her sweater, as she petted him until he relaxed into her hold and began to purr. "It's okay, Manchu. No more flying. No more intruders. We're safe now."

His little face scrunched up, but he bunted his head against her chin.

A tap on the door and Louis poked his head in. Manchu yowled, scrambled out of her arms and fled into the en suite bathroom.

"Sorry." He dropped her bags inside the doorway. "I thought I'd bring you his supplies so he could get settled."

"Thanks, Louis. I'm so sorry about this. I'm sure the last thing your brother wanted was a cat loose in his home."

"Gabriel doesn't live here. This suite belongs to the p— Wolf Enterprises. So don't you worry about my brother."

"If you're sure?"

"Set him up in the bathroom, and, Melinda, take your time. It's been a rough twelve hours for both of you."

Louis disappeared and she listened to his footsteps on the stairs, not sure if she was grateful for this moment alone, this chance to gather her thoughts, or not. Too many images of the scene in her flat kept flashing through her mind, held at bay until now by her awareness of the sexy, hot, gorgeous — every positive attribute, every cliche you could use to physically describe men — twins.

Now she was alone, she had nothing to distract her and all she could think about was the man standing over her with a gun. The blurred visual of Louis' head, but not Louis' head. Not a *man's* head. The way he'd torn apart the intruder's throat. With his *teeth*. She couldn't stop playing it over and over. Couldn't stop the speculation, the strange explanations her mind offered for what she'd witnessed.

Trauma had a way of distorting things in your mind. She'd experienced it before. Night after night she'd lain in her bed, the vision of her father's rage distorted face like some sort of monstrous gargoyle. Hideous and huge, he towered in her mind, a threat to both her and her mother. It wasn't until she was older, until she'd left home, she'd realized he wasn't that tall, that big and was nothing more than an ordinary-looking man. The ugliness was on the inside. Her childish mind had embellished. Created an image of what her father *should* look like.

Perhaps she'd seen Louis as a wolf because she wanted to view him as a protector. That was the only reasonable explanation. She needed to keep busy. Not think too much. Or she would convince herself those images, those fragments of distorted memory, were real. That Louis had shifted into some kind of part human, part...wolf. Which was ridiculous.

Melinda snatched up the bag. Manchu had got her through many a tough time, sleeping beside her, keeping the nightmares of her childhood at bay. Focusing on Manchu would get her through this.

In the en suite, a room bigger than the kitchen in her London flat, with a shower the size of her entire bathroom, she sorted through the supplies, laying them out on the vanity — cat litter, food and water bowls, a litter tray, tins of cat food, her phone, her purse. That would come in handy. She unzipped it and peered inside. Her wallet and two thumb drives.

She'd need to get a new sim card for her phone, but she was glad to see those thumb drives. And to have her laptop. She'd made sure she'd had a visual of it at all times since this morning. She might be paying the twins as her bodyguards, expecting them to live up to their end of the bargain, and having them around did make her feel safer, but that didn't mean she trusted them. Not completely. Not yet.

And... Melinda peered into the bag. There, in the bottom, wrapped in a tea towel, was her mother's teapot, along with two tins of jasmine tea. She reached in, cradling the teapot, her throat tight and tears pricking her eyes. Whatever had possessed Pierre to pack it, Melinda didn't care. She had her teapot. The one thing she had left of her mother, other than her memories.

She hugged it to her chest. *Thank you, Pierre.*

Placing the teapot back in the bag, she set up a litter tray in the corner for Manchu, and food and water bowls down by the door. With Manchu sorted, Melinda needed to get on to the task she was here for. With an eye on the open door of the suite, she sat on the bed, opened her Tor browser, logged into the dark web and sent a message to MysticMage.

Chapter Sixteen

Louis tromped down the floating staircase. She'd said thank you, *Louis*. With such certainty, as though she knew he *was* Louis and *not* Pierre. Thank you, *Louis*. Not *thanks*, or *hey, you*, like many a woman had before her because they couldn't tell them apart. Maybe Pierre was right. Maybe she *was* different from the other women. Because she was their mate.

It warmed his heart a little after this morning. After the way she'd scrambled from the bed within moments of waking, as though she regretted what had happened between them. Not the emotion he—nor Pierre, he suspected—were hoping for after their intimacy.

He wouldn't apologize for what they'd done. She'd needed it. So had they. They'd only just found her and they'd come so close to losing her. He'd needed to hold her, lose himself in her, and forget about that split second when he'd entered her office to a man standing over her, pistol raised and aimed at her head. If they'd been but a minute later...

They hadn't been, and she was here. Thank whatever god, universe, or fates who were watching out for them. And she'd agreed to keep them around as her bodyguards. He was fine with letting her think she was paying them—if it made her more comfortable with the arrangement—but he had no intention of backing off. If she asked them to or not. Ever.

He entered the kitchen to Pierre making *café*, filling Gabe and Stef in on the last few weeks. Pierre handed him a cup. He would have killed for a pastry, something sweet, but for now this would do.

Stef, her hip cocked against the island bench, eyeballed the two of them. "A cat? You remember you're both werewolves, right? And, in time, she will be, too."

"*Oui*." Cats and dogs were naturally antagonistic. A cat and werewolves—that would take a bit of finessing.

She shook her head, a bemused expression on her face. "Well, this is going to be interesting."

Louis rubbed his hand over the back of his neck and grimaced. "We've got a few issues to sort out before we get to that point. That's the least of them."

She'd left her home and her country. Pierre had made the right decision bringing her cat along.

Gabe stilled, his cup halfway to his mouth. "She doesn't know?"

"What we are? Or that the client she believes is a battered wife on the run from her abusive husband is really a time-traveling old witch who sent a hitman to kill her?" Louis gulped down a mouthful of coffee Pierre had added a heap of sugar to. The sweetness didn't detract from the sharp edge of their predicament.

Gabe shook his head. "For two people so smart, you've made a pig's breakfast of this."

Pierre snorted. "Like things went smoothly with you and Annabelle."

"While we're talking about fuck ups," said Louis, "what's with us using this place again? The views are great, but Cordelia has to know it exists after what went down over Christmas. If she does, you can bet the Faucherians do, too. If we're going with the animal analogies, we're like sitting ducks here."

He didn't like that at all. Not with their vulnerable mate here.

"The Ritz-Carlton has undergone a few changes in the last few months," said Gabe, throwing back the last bit of his *café* and rinsing his cup in the sink. "We put the word out among our friends that we have a vested interest in this place. A good portion of the employees, from management down to the cleaning staff, are now friendly to us. And there are wards everywhere. Especially here. Annabelle's coven saw to that. Can't you feel them?"

Of course he could. The subtle hum hadn't let up since the moment they'd walked into the foyer. Would it be enough to keep their enemies at bay, and Melinda safe?

The distant swish of the elevator doors had both him and Pierre on high alert. He sniffed the air. Food— spicy—and female shifter. A statuesque blonde smothered in his brother's scent breezed into the kitchen, bags of takeout in her hands. This must be Annabelle, their brother's mate.

"Ooh, double trouble," she said, placing the bags on the counter. "From Gabe's descriptions, you must be Pierre," she said, jerking her chin at his twin. "And you must be Louis. We got your text." She opened a bag and slid a container over to him. "Here's what you asked for. Shacha noodles, with spicy sausage, tofu and vegetables. Oddly specific. I take it, it's for —"

Melinda entered the kitchen, her laptop under her arm. They'd have to pry that thing away from her to get her to use *les toilettes.* She'd probably try to sleep with the thing. Ever since this morning, on the plane, she'd kept it close. She'd suspected Pierre of trying to access it. Smart little cipher. She wasn't wrong, but her mistrust stung all the same.

"I've contacted my client to arrange a meetup."

"Where?" asked Pierre.

She swung her gaze to him, and beneath the suspicion a hint of something else, a softening.

Her laptop announced an incoming message. She flipped the lid, tapped the keyboard. "Dogpatch?"

He looked to Annabelle for clarification.

"It's on the eastern side of the city, near the waterfront," said Annabelle. "It used to be mostly industrial, but it's changed a lot in the last twenty years. Now it's kind of a mix of both. It's about twenty minutes by car from here."

"Do you need backup?" asked Gabe. "In case you run into any more hitmen."

If Cordelia had Faucherians guarding her, Gabe and Stef would be an asset. If she used spells, if she had other members of the King family with her — witches and warlocks, all of them — they were going to need Annabelle, and perhaps a few members of her coven.

Melinda shook her head. "No. I agreed to two bodyguards. No more. My client will be terrified as it is. I can't show up with a bunch of people."

"We'll hang back and keep out of sight." Gabriel held up his hands. "We'll be there if you need us, that's all."

Melinda glanced around the kitchen, the designer kitchen with its high-end appliances. "Thanks, but I don't think I can afford that."

Stef's eyebrows shot up.

Gabe's forehead bunched in a frown, his gaze swiveling between him and Pierre, and his gut tightened at the censure in his brother's eyes. "You're taking money from her? To protect her?"

"No!" He denied in unison with his twin.

"Yes!" Melinda rounded on them both. "We agreed."

Oui, they had, but only to appease her. His brother had to know that.

Gabriel shrugged. "*D'accord*. You have an agreement, but I won't be charging you, Melinda. I'll take it out of my brothers' hides on the training mats if I have to."

Louis groaned. "Trust me, Melinda. Gabe will get his due. He won't go easy on us because he's our brother. He's a big *connard* and neither of us, not even if Pierre and I work together, have defeated him yet."

Pierre rubbed his ribs. "I still have bruises from last time. From before Christmas."

Gabe grinned. "Sure, you do."

"You should come and watch, Melinda," said Stefanie, winking at their mate. "Hot and sweaty men, naked from the waist up, pounding on each other. Mm-mm."

"Count me in," said Annabelle.

Louis rolled his eyes. They didn't need their help seducing their mate. Or maybe they did. With what was bound to go down today, they could use all the help they could get. Including the backup his brother was offering.

"Stay close, but out of sight," Pierre said to Gabe. "We may not need you, but who knows what resources we're up against. And we don't want to spook Melinda's client. If she runs, we may never find her. Melinda, when does your client want to meet?"

"In an hour."

Louis slid the container of steaming-hot takeout across the bench and handed her a fork. "Plenty of time. We skipped breakfast. You need to eat first."

Melinda pried the lid off the container. She glanced up, a question in her eyes.

"Shacha noodles, just how you like them."

Vulnerability flashed across her face. "They're my favorite. How did you…?"

Louis rounded the counter and tucked a stray lock of hair behind her ear. "The day we ran into you in the elevator. Remember?"

That softening in her eyes again, this time directed at him.

"Thank you, Louis."

Louis. Again, she'd identified the correct twin. He shared a look with his brother. Hope flared in Pierre's eyes. If they could neutralize Cordelia, if Melinda were to see her client for who, what, she truly was… They would still have one challenge, but they would have time to woo their little mate, let her get to know them, come to trust them before the big reveal. The situation was salvageable.

Chapter Seventeen

Pierre surveyed the dilapidated building from down the street. Dogpatch was indeed a mix of industrial and residential, as Annabelle had described. At the other end was a row of million-dollar condos with water views. This end had yet to be gentrified. A few abandoned dock warehouses remained, surrounded by chain-link fencing with Keep Out signs at intervals, faced off with disused mooring points and wharfs jutting into the San Francisco Bay. Except for a stray dog picking through rubbish, the place appeared deserted.

Melinda's unease tickled his senses. They'd done an online search on the address before they'd left the penthouse, and dug into the sale records. The building *was* listed as owned by a Robert King. A man who, he'd discovered with a little digging, had died in nineteen seventy-six and whose sudden resurrection this morning didn't come as a surprise. According to Annabelle, Cordelia didn't have a husband. Lots of family, who she ruled over with ruthless authority, but no husband. It was a running joke in the coven she'd mated with the devil himself, and her progeny were the spawn of hell.

The Robert King identity was flimsy—a rush job. He'd cracked it in minutes. By silent agreement between him, his twin and Gabe, they hadn't told Melinda. There was a chance Cordelia would be there. A small chance, but they had nothing else to go on.

Melinda peered through the car's windscreen. "Are we sure this is the building?"

The satellite view hadn't come close to conveying the emptiness, the abandoned air that hung over the four warehouses in front of them. She flipped open her laptop and double checked the address. "This is it. The address she gave me."

If she'd wanted to call a halt to this, to turn around and go back to the penthouse suite, he wouldn't have blamed her. Instead, she squared her shoulders and stepped out of the car. She might be slight, and barely reach their shoulders, but their little mate had courage and determination packed into that tiny body of hers.

The crisp bay air hit him as he stepped out onto the bitumen, and Pierre opened up his senses. No hint of a ward, but there was something else. A slight deadening of sensation he'd come to associate with the presence of wolfsbane. Faucherians? Maybe. But Cordelia had to know of their weaknesses, too.

Wolfsbane, the curse of their existence. An herb with a pretty purple flower, it had a devastating impact on werewolves. Unlike humans, they didn't have to ingest it to feel its effects. In small doses, it dulled their senses, neutralizing the advantage they had over humans. In larger quantities, it took away any control they had over their form. They would continue to shift from human to wolf and back again until they escaped the presence of the herb. Or until their body used up all energy and they died.

The warehouse was a trap. Of course it was. They'd known it would be. The only one who thought differently was Melinda.

He uncuffed the leather band from around his wrist, flipped it over and reattached it, putting the silver wolf against his skin. It burned, no more than one of Louis' hot trays fresh from the oven, but a burn and a blistering of skin all the same. It wouldn't heal until he turned the cuff back over.

Silver, another threat to his kind. Silver restraints, though softer and weaker than steel, would bind their wolves, incapacitating them. It'd happened to Ulrik Voclain, Laurent's ancestor. The small amount on their cuffs, however, counteracted the effects of wolfsbane.

Pierre tested his senses. He grinned. As sharp as ever.

Louis rounded the car, his cuff inverted, too. "Let's do this."

In a car tucked into an alleyway down the street, waited Gabe and Annabelle. Invisible to him except for their scent were members of Annabelle's coven, hidden around the abandoned dock. They hadn't told Melinda about them, and he hoped she'd have no need to ever find out they'd been there, but he was glad they were. If they were to encounter Cordelia, if she turned up in person, they were going to need them.

Would she, though? Or had she sent the Faucherians in alone? Like she had in London.

His phone vibrated. Gabe.

Annabelle says there are no wards she can detect.

He sent a thumbs-up emoji.

Be careful in there. It's a trap.

He snorted. Way to state the obvious, brother. He turned to Melinda. "Are you ready?"

She wiped her sweaty palms on her jeans and nodded.

"Glad you hired us on as bodyguards now?" teased Louis.

Pierre punched his brother on the arm. Louis feigned an injury.

"Knock it off, *tête de noeud.*" Pierre scowled at his twin. "Can you not be serious for once?"

Melinda jerked her head at the warehouse. "Let's get this over with. If my client's in that building, I don't want her to have to hide here for any longer than is necessary. I want to get her somewhere safe."

The only safe place for Cordelia was six feet under. Safe for everyone else, that was. This witch may have messed with his ancestors, but her time was fast running out. The Langeais wolves were not tenth-century chevaliers anymore. They'd adapted well over the centuries. One little old lady, no matter how powerful, would not prevail against them.

Melinda took a few steps toward the building.

Pierre grabbed her arm and pulled her back into the shadows. "Wait."

The chain-link gate hung open, making a mockery of the security fence and its Keep Out signs. An open invitation.

Pierre pulled a pair of bolt cutters from the backpack slung over his shoulder and handed them to Louis.

"We go in the back way. No point announcing our presence."

Understanding flickered in her eyes. "You think this is a trap?"

His nostrils flared at her innocence. How had she survived this long with clients like Cordelia? It made him want to scoop her up and take her far away from here. Keep her safe, protected. But their determined little mate would never allow it. "I think it's wise to take precautions. Anyone could be watching us, from inside the building or out."

Flanking Melinda, they crossed the deserted dock two warehouses down from their target. With a snick of the bolt cutters, Louis cut a hole in the security fencing, peeled the wire back and crawled through.

"You think her husband might be tailing me to get to my client?"

Pierre helped Melinda through the hole. No. No one had followed them, of that he was sure. Their greatest danger lay inside the warehouse. "It's always a possibility." Pierre pulled himself through the gap in the fence. "We'll get you to your client, Melinda. Trust us."

Melinda surveyed their surroundings, peering into the shadows as though what hid in them might reveal itself to her. She didn't have their eyesight, their hearing or their sense of smell. She couldn't know what lay in wait inside the building. Yet, had they not been on hand, she would have attempted this on her own. Had they not targeted her to get to Cordelia, perhaps she wouldn't be in this position in the first place. Then they would not have met their mate.

"Come on. Let's go find this client of yours. I hope she's worth it."

The passion of her crusade burned in her eyes. It was a shame, in this instance, it was misplaced. It was going to hurt when she discovered the truth.

With Louis leading the way and Pierre bringing up the rear, the three of them crept from building to building, the bolt cutters making quick work of the security fencing, until they came to the one they wanted. At the door, Louis paused and held his finger to his lips. He tested the knob, then gave a wrench, the snapping of the lock an explosion of sound in the dead air. The scent of disused warehouse, damp, and animal feces hit him, but no humans. *Strange. Witchcraft?* He sent off a quick text to Gabe, alerting him, before following Louis and Melinda into the dark and silent warehouse.

He kneeled beside Melinda, hidden behind a stack of empty steel barrels, scanning the interior. Above them, muted light filtered through the grimy windows, revealing a large, almost empty space. At the other end of the building, a staircase led to an office on a mezzanine level. A rusty shutter banged in the breeze whipped up off the bay. A bird flapped, disturbed from its roost, before settling. Again, no sign of any humans. But they were there. The low hum tickling his senses confirmed his suspicions. Witchcraft. The old witch, or one of her many descendants?

Louis turned to him, a wicked grin on his face. He pointed to a space darker than the rest of the warehouse, almost impenetrable to their enhanced vision. Almost, but not quite. There, hidden within the swirls of inky darkness, he caught the hint of white hair. The old witch had come. Stupid or supremely arrogant and confident in her own power. Now honed in on her, it was hard to miss the tap of the rubber tipped cane on the cement floor and the slide of aged feet. Hatred blazed in a pair of eyes—one blue, one green.

Cordelia had the gift of second sight. Had she foreseen this moment? Chosen Melinda because she knew it would lead them to this point? Had this trap been months in the making? With wolfsbane in play, this trap wasn't for Melinda alone.

Chapter Eighteen

Melinda couldn't fathom a little old lady using this derelict warehouse as a hideout. She rubbed at her sternum. That bad feeling was back again. Could her client's husband have paid his hacker to infiltrate her IRC? Not beyond the bounds of possibility. She hadn't forgotten the malware. If his efforts hadn't been directed at her, if it hadn't ended with a tattooed hired killer breaking into her apartment, she might have admired his skill.

Lord almighty, what was she doing here? Skulking around abandoned warehouses, playing out a scene from a thriller movie? She stared down at her empty hands. Weaponless. If Pierre and Louis were carrying any, they hadn't drawn them. What were they *thinking*? She was so out of her depth she might as well be at the bottom of the Mariana Trench.

Despite her qualms and her mind screaming at her to retreat, she stayed put, crouched beside Louis and Pierre, glad of their comforting presence. Her self-appointed bodyguards. That she was paying. Probably *huge* sums of money.

Was her client here at all? Oh, God. What if... What if her client's husband's goons had been and gone, taking his wife with him? Melinda's mother had never attempted to leave her father. The shame of it, the fear of how the community would view her for not being the dutiful, submissive wife expected of her. Raised in a different era, her mother had clung to the old ways, her tradition, her culture.

If her mother *had* left, *had* escaped from the hell of her marriage, Melinda could only imagine being dragged back into it would have been devastating.

Movement caught her eye—a shape, small and hunched, edging out of the shadows. The tap-tap of something on the cement floor. Melinda squinted. There, a woman bent over, using a cane for support. *Shit.* The woman was frailer than she'd thought. Yet she'd had the strength and the courage to leave her abusive husband, dive into the dark web, and hide out in this place. If Melinda were in her position, would she have done the same?

"L-three-six-four-CY. Is that you?"

L364CY. Legacy. Her username. That MysticMage spoke the numerals—didn't understand what the numbers signified—confirmed Melinda's suspicion that she wasn't a regular user of the dark web. She was lucky she'd found Melinda. No other hacker would go to these extremes to protect their client, or make certain the new identities they'd created held.

"Is anyone there?"

The voice was frail, with a nervous quiver. The poor woman. Melinda half rose to go to her, but Pierre held her back.

"Wait," the words whispered against her ear. "Not alone."

She nodded, and as one, the three of them stepped out from behind the barrels, Louis and Pierre using their bodies as a shield.

The old woman squinted at them. "L-three-six-four-CY? Is that you?"

"Yes, MysticMage. It's me. Legacy. L-three-six-four-CY." She tried to shoulder her way to the front, but Pierre growled at her.

The old woman smiled. "You've brought your friends with you."

"Yes, these are the friends I told you about. They've come to help me get you to safety. Don't be afraid. You can trust them. It's your husband you're running from, isn't it? I know you didn't say, but..." The signs were there. She knew them well.

"Oh, thank goodness." The woman clutched a hand to her chest, edging forward, leaning heavily on her cane. "I've been so frightened. I— Oh!"

Eight men slunk out of the shadows. Louis growled low in his throat, a sound more animal than human. He pressed closer to her. They both did.

"Are these men with you, dear?"

Melinda swallowed. They were surrounded by men in tactical gear. Armed men, their guns pointing at them, and at MysticMage. On each of them, the dark hint of ink on their necks. In better light, she'd no doubt she'd find the tattoo was an elaborate F with crossed swords. The same as the one on the intruder in her apartment.

"No." Melinda clutched at Pierre. "These men aren't with us."

Then something happened that would forever live in her mind, in her nightmares. With a roar loud enough to bring down the rusted tin roof and send all the birds roosting in the rafters into panicked flight, Pierre changed. Right before her eyes. So did Louis.

Their clothing ripped and their bodies contorted. Fur sprouted, and within a blink of an eye, the men she knew were gone, replaced by two very large black wolves. Melinda screamed.

What had been Pierre but was now a beast launched itself at an armed man, taking him down, ripping his throat out. Guns went off, and a large weight knocked her to the ground. A beast with wicked teeth and a gaping maw. Through her haze of terror, she glimpsed MysticMage being dragged away by two armed tattooed men, her cane falling to the floor. *No!*

She tried to get to her feet, to go after them, but the beast grabbed her clothing in his teeth and dragged her back toward the barrels as bullets whizzed by. The wolf let go of her, letting out a roar filled with pain and fury. Those eyes. Hazel, with a hint of mischief despite the situation. Louis, but not a Louis she'd ever expected to encounter. What the hell *was* he? She scrambled backward. He nodded once then, bleeding from a wound to his shoulder, he joined the fray.

Melinda scampered between the rows of steel barrows, the ping of bullets against them sending her deeper into their midst. Another roar. Another injured wolf, or the same one? Louis and Pierre. Wolves. Beasts. Not human. And MysticMage gone. Taken by the men her husband had hired. *Oh God. Oh God. Oh God.* She'd be lucky to get out of this alive.

More bullets pinged off the barrels. Melinda crouched between two of them, her hands over her ears, her body shaking and tears streaming unchecked down her face. The job she did was dangerous. She knew that. Her clients, all of them, were hiding from something, or someone, but never in a million years had she imagined it would lead to this. To a shootout in an abandoned warehouse. Highly trained and well-equipped men facing off with two…two…*werewolves.*

She rocked, her choked sobs drowned out by the battle around her. Until they weren't. Until her keening was the only sound in a silent warehouse.

Melinda clamped her mouth shut. What was happening? Were they all dead? Louis? Pierre? Would they turn on her now? Her chest was so tight she struggled to breathe.

Melinda listened. Not a sound. She peered through a gap between the barrels. An arm, flung out, unmoving, lay at the very edge of the stack of barrels. A human arm, not covered in fur. A hand, not a paw. Above the wrist, a watch. Not a Roger Dubious Excalibur. Her relief at that discovery had her wanting to flee. But she had to know.

She crept forward, one silent step at a time, to the next barrel. Her hands flush against its cool surface, she peered around it. Vacant blue eyes stared at her, unseeing. She jumped back, her breathing shallow and her heart racing. She snuck another look. The hand belonged to one of the tattooed men, dead now. She didn't focus on his throat, the blood and gore. She could barely look past his sightless eyes.

Melinda moved to the next barrel. Another body in tactical gear came into view, a gun beside his leg. She'd never fired a weapon. Never held one, but it seemed like a good idea to have one in her hands right now.

Melinda inched forward. In the silence, strange cracking and popping sounds. *Oh, God.* Could the werewolves, the beasts she'd once known as men, be...be...devouring their kills?

A door slammed behind her. Melinda gave up on stealth and dove for the gun. Her shaky hands locked around the grip and, on legs wobblier than Jell-O, she rose. She swung the gun from one threat to the next.

What the actual fuck?

Not a single tattooed man remained standing. From the amount of blood, she was sure none of them had survived. What she faced, what her brain was having trouble comprehending, were the three naked men standing before her. Louis, Pierre and Gabriel.

Chapter Nineteen

Louis dropped the bullet he'd dug out of his shoulder, and held up his hands. "Easy, now, Melinda. Put the gun down."

She swung his way, a shaky finger on the trigger, and he stared down the barrel. The bullet wouldn't kill him — unless she got off a lucky shot and nailed him in the head — but it would hurt like hell. Fucking Faucherians and their silver-coated bullets.

She stared at him, then Pierre, the horror in her eyes all but wrenching his heart from his chest. Their mate was afraid of them. He looked around at the carnage on the floor — throats ripped out, gaping wounds. One guy was missing a hand. It lay curled around the grip of a pistol. Neither he nor Pierre were unscathed. Covered in the blood of their enemies as well as their own. The wound in his shoulder was healing. Pierre's wound in his thigh was a through and through. Gabriel, the *connard*, had come out of the fight uninjured, his face, neck and chest splattered with blood, none of it his. He couldn't blame Melinda for being scared.

Annabelle stepped forward. "Maybe I should —"

She froze as Melinda spun the pistol in her direction. Gabriel roared and leaped, shielding his mate. Before Louis could utter a word, Melinda fired. The shot went wide.

"Melinda." He took a step toward her.

"Stop." Melinda gripped the pistol tighter, her attention skittering between them all. "Don't come any closer." She half sobbed. "I will shoot you if I have to."

"Melinda, it's me. Louis. We're not going to hurt you."

"We're your bodyguards, remember? You're paying us to protect you," said Pierre, his voice soft, soothing, though Louis sensed the turmoil and the pain his brother held in check.

She spun to face his twin. "I don't know who...what you are anymore."

"We're still the same Louis and Pierre who invited you to our apartment for drinks." He inched forward. She swung the barrel at him again. He gave her his best friendly smile. "You liked my nuts, remember?"

If they could just talk her down, get her in their arms and reassure her she was safe... "We flew all the way from London with you. If we wanted to hurt you, we had every opportunity. You let us touch you then. Comfort you. More than comfort. The three of us."

Her hands dipped a little. They nearly had her.

Behind the barrels, Stef moved on silent feet, sneaking up on Melinda.

"Wait," he called out, but it was too late.

Stef clamped a hand around Melinda's wrist. Their mate screamed and struggled. The gun went off, the bullet plowing into the warehouse roof. Then Stef had control of the weapon. She removed the magazine and the cartridge from the chamber and tossed it aside.

Melinda backed away from them all, her eyes wide. "Who are you people? Are you all…?" She cackled, on the verge of hysteria. "Wolf Enterprises. I should've guessed. How could I have guessed? Who in their right mind would believe people could turn into…animals?"

Animals? The word sucker punched him in the chest. She thought them animals, now?

Annabelle held up a backpack, tossing it to them. "Why don't you boys go get cleaned up, put some clothes on and go wait with the cars? Melinda, Stef and I are going to have a little talk, woman to woman."

Louis growled his displeasure. She was their mate, and she was afraid. She needed them. The urge to protect her, comfort her, to tell her everything was going to be all right, burned within him. But would it be? Right now, she wanted to run from them, from what they were. To lock it away in the back of her mind and pretend she'd never seen what she had. He could smell it on her.

He took a step toward her, and Melinda backed away, her bottom lip quivering. His heart cracked wide open at the look in her eyes.

"Thank you, Annabelle. Perhaps that's for the best. For now." Pierre put a steadying hand on his shoulder. "Come, Louis."

The ride back to the Ritz-Carlton was a somber one. How Annabelle and Stef talked Melinda into returning with them, he didn't know, but there must've been some heavy persuasion. Convincing her to ride in the car with them was out of the question, so the girls took one car, and Pierre, Gabe and he drove back in the other.

In the foyer, they parted ways. The women heading for the bar, while they took the elevator to the penthouse suite. She looked at them then, as they stood in the elevator waiting for the door to close. Her face pale and tear-stained, the terror gone from her eyes, replaced by bewilderment and a good measure of shock. Worlds away from last night as they'd fucked her fear away. Now they were what frightened her.

In their suite, Pierre poured them all a glass of whiskey. Gabriel flopped on the sofa and Pierre stood by the window, looking out at the San Francisco skyline. Louis downed his glass in one gulp, the burn of the spirit doing nothing to quench the pain in his chest. He poured himself another.

"Well, that went as well as we could have expected," said Gabe.

Louis rounded on his brother. "As well as we could have expected? Our mate is afraid of us. Cordelia has escaped. There are six dead bodies in an otherwise empty warehouse by the docks. Worse, Cordelia played the part of the poor little old lady to perfection. Melinda still believes her client is in danger. Not *the* danger!" He was yelling now, his hand fisted around the crystal glass so tight it might shatter. "Our mate thinks *we're* the danger."

"Louis—"

"No! Don't Louis me, Pierre!" He hurled his glass at the wall. It shattered, crystal and whiskey spraying over the wall and the cream carpet. Louis slumped down on the sofa, his head in his hands. "What if...?" He raised his head to meet the anguish in Pierre's eyes. "What if she wants nothing to do with us now?" He raked his hand through his hair. "Look at us. We're already trying to drink away our pain."

Pierre turned away. His brother always did like to mask his feelings, but they throbbed in the air, more powerful than an electromagnetic pulse. His brother was hurting as much as he was.

Gabe leaned forward, his elbows on his knees. "Don't give up, Louis." He swiveled to include Pierre. "Either of you. Remember, I thought I'd lost Annabelle. Three long years without her almost killed me. Then look what happened. Now, here I am. Mated. Fate will find a way."

Louis was glad Gabe had omitted the 'happily' bit. He didn't think he could face it if he hadn't.

Pierre grunted. "Tell that to Maxime."

"Have a little faith. In Stef and Annabelle. In your mate. She's had a shock. It's not the way any of us would want our mates finding out what we are, I'll grant you, but she'll come around. Just give her some time. A lot happened in that warehouse. She's going to need to come to grips with it all, to assimilate it."

Maybe.

"Louis," said Gabe. "She's smart, right? Stupid-smart, like you two."

Oui, she was. Their malware had only got them so far. She hadn't made it easy for them to track her down.

"And you've done nothing but protect her. You saved her from the Faucherian sent to kill her. You protected her at the warehouse. Killed for her. She'll join the dots. Once she's had a bit of time to think about it."

"Gabe's right, Louis. We need to give her time."

Time? They'd be lucky if she ever wanted to be in the same room with them again. Accepting she was their mate? Convincing her to bind herself to them forever? To become one of them? Right now, they'd have more chance hacking the fucking Pentagon.

Chapter Twenty

Melinda sipped on the colorful cocktail Stefanie had placed in front of her, not really tasting it. She hoped it had a kick to it. After what she'd witnessed in the warehouse, she was going to need something stronger than juice and syrup. Something to blanket her thoughts with a numbing buzz, preventing her from replaying the horrific scene over and over in her mind.

The statuesque blonde, the one she'd shot at but who seemed to bear her no ill will for it, ended her call and joined them, sliding onto the bar stool. "I'm Annabelle, by the way. Gabriel's mate. In all the planning and stuff in the penthouse, we didn't get introduced."

Gabriel's *mate*? Oh. Like a wife, but...werewolf style. *Oh, God. We're going there. We're doing this.* She didn't want to, but there was no denying what had happened in that warehouse. Louis and Pierre had...*changed*. Become beasts. Wolves. She hadn't imagined it in her London flat. It was real.

"Are you…?" Melinda's gaze ping-ponged between Stef and Annabelle.

Stefanie cocked an eyebrow. "You can say it, Melinda. Speak it out loud."

Melinda gulped. "Are you…werewolves?" She kept her voice low. They'd chosen a table in a quiet corner, away from the bar, but Melinda didn't want to risk anyone overhearing. They'd think she was insane. She wasn't sure she wasn't.

Stefanie patted her arm. "There you go. That wasn't so hard, was it? In answer to your question, yes, we are. Annabelle is also a witch."

Annabelle nodded. "I am. I'm the High Priestess of the San Francisco Bay coven."

A *witch*? No. This was too bizarre for words. What had her life come to? She longed to be back in London, in front of her screens with Manchu on her lap, locked behind her walls of security, where the worst she would encounter was the likes of JohnnyBeGood and his not so good deeds. Instead, she was sitting here drinking cocktails with two women who professed to be werewolves. One of whom also claimed to be a witch.

Annabelle clasped Melinda's hand and gave it a gentle squeeze. "I know this is all really hard for you right now. It's a lot to take in. And I know Louis and Pierre wouldn't have wanted you to find out this way, but they didn't have any choice. If they hadn't shifted…"

Annabelle left the words hanging there. Men with guns had surrounded them. Them and… MysticMage!

"My client." In all of this, she'd forgotten about her client. The scene at the warehouse flashed into her mind. The frail woman she knew as MysticMage struggling against two men as they dragged her from the warehouse. "The poor woman. She must be terrified. I have to…" She made to get up.

Stefanie placed a hand on her shoulder, keeping her in her seat. "I'm sure the boys are already working on an angle to find her. There's nothing you can do for her right now."

And the twins… *Oh, God.* They were hurt, bleeding. "But Louis took a bullet to the shoulder, and Pierre had one in his thigh. They shouldn't be working on anything. They need to be in a hospital receiving medical care."

Annabelle squeezed her hand again. "They'll be fine. Their bodies were already healing before we left the warehouse. It's a werewolf thing. There's not much that will kill them. Us."

Melinda rubbed her forehead and took another long sip of her drink. A werewolf thing? She'd need a few more of these cocktails before *that* would sound normal.

"You said Louis was shot in the shoulder and Pierre in the thigh. You can tell them apart?" asked Stefanie.

Melinda drained her glass, a slight buzz developing in her brain. "Can't you?"

Stefanie shared a look with Annabelle. "We can, but no human ever has."

Melinda shrugged. "I don't know how anyone could confuse them. They're completely different—their personalities, their mannerisms, the way they walk." She found herself smiling, remembering. "Louis likes his pastries. Pierre likes his coffee. Louis is messy. Pierre is obsessively neat. Louis is all charm and teasing. Pierre's the serious one, the one in charge. Always responsible." A flush of heat swept through her body. "Louis wears boxer briefs. Pierre likes to go commando."

"Okay." Annabelle held up her hands. "That's more information than I needed to know about my brothers-in-law."

Stefanie chuckled. "I think the rum in the mai tai might be kicking in."

Annabelle scanned the QR code on the menu. "I'll order us another round." She glanced over her shoulder at a woman heading for their corner of the room. "And while we wait for it, let me introduce you to someone."

The woman, curvy with a pallor to her bronze skin, slipped onto the stool beside Melinda. Dark shadows lined her eyes, but her smile was warm and friendly.

"Melinda, this is Isobella, my sister," said Annabelle. "She's a witch, like me, but she's not a werewolf. I thought you might like the perspective of someone who isn't a shifter, but who knows plenty of them and about them. Now, ask your questions, and we will answer them as best we can." Her grin was cheeky. "And I'm sure Stef has more than a few interesting tales to tell about Louis and Pierre."

* * * *

With an encyclopedia's worth of knowledge about werewolves and witches she never dreamed of knowing when she awoke this morning, Melinda entered the penthouse suite. Annabelle, Stefanie and Isobella had seen her to the suite's lobby. Ensuring she made it there and didn't flee out into the San Franciscan spring night, she suspected.

Gabriel rose from the sofa. "This is my cue to leave." Reaching her in the doorway, he paused. "Don't be too hard on them, Melinda. They would have died for you today."

Died for her? According to Annabelle, Stefanie and Isobella, that was no easy feat. Not much killed a werewolf. Beheading, bleeding out from too many wounds before healing could begin, a silver bullet to the brain. All gruesome, violent deaths.

The door closed behind Gabriel, and Melinda was alone with Louis and Pierre. Lights twinkled over the city, framing Pierre. His face was a picture of controlled calm as he sipped at a glass of whiskey. If she knew anything about Pierre, he'd be a cauldron of emotions beneath the surface.

On the wall, a whiskey stain and shattered glass beneath it on the floor. Louis. He sat on the sofa, his knees bouncing in rapid motion. They both stared at her, waiting. She couldn't do this right now.

"I'm going to check on Manchu, and maybe take a shower."

"It's late," said Pierre. "The main suite is yours. Louis will sleep in the second bedroom, and I'll take the sofa. You have nothing to fear from us, Melinda."

All she could manage was a nod before she fled up the floating staircase.

Manchu unfurled himself from his position in the middle of the bed and padded over to greet her. His purr, the rub of his head against her as she cradled him in her arms, gave her some comfort. But not enough. Downstairs, two werewolves…what…waited? Raged? Hurt? Yes. They were hurting. And waiting. And hoping. For her to come to grips with what she'd seen. Annabelle and Stef hadn't touched too much on Louis and Pierre, in fact they'd steered the conversation away from them a few times, but she'd garnered that much from their conversation.

Melinda stripped off her clothes and immersed herself beneath the shower, the opulence of the room lost on her tonight. While the water washed away any grime from the warehouse, it did nothing to ease her thoughts or soothe the turmoil in her mind.

Melinda didn't know how long she stood beneath the spray—long enough for the pleasant numbness of two mai tais to wear off—but when she stepped out, she'd made a decision. She couldn't hide away from this. She had to confront it sooner or later. It might as well be now.

Her mind shied away from what they were, but her heart told her Pierre had spoken true. She had nothing to fear from them. If they'd wanted to hurt her, they could have done so long before now. They'd done nothing but protect her, care for her. She eyed Manchu curled up in the middle of the huge bed. Hell, they'd helped her get her cat here, though Manchu had been a spitting ball of orange fur the whole time.

Knowing what they were, his behavior made more sense now. Manchu had recognized they were werewolves from the moment he'd set eyes on them. Now she, too, knew the truth.

Dressed in clean clothes, her hair still damp, she took a tremulous breath and headed down the stairs.

Chapter Twenty-One

Pierre unpacked the items from the bag he'd snuck up to get while Melinda was in the shower. The clay teapot and a tin of jasmine tea. Whatever meaning she attributed to it, it soothed her. Something from her childhood, perhaps. On the grainy black-and-white security feed—a poor substitute for the real thing—every time she'd made tea her body would visibly relax. The tension would ease from her shoulders and the worry would slip from her face, replaced by a serene calm and a wistful smile.

Today had been a shock for her. Pierre would have given anything not to have revealed their true nature to her that way, but surrounded by armed men, they'd had no choice. He'd risk everything, even losing her, to keep her safe. Louis, too.

Louis dumped the shards of the crystal glass that had borne his frustration into the trash. "Do you think she'll come around?"

Pierre shrugged. "I don't know."

"Well, if she does, I think we should tell her."

"Tell her?" Pierre drew in a breath. He knew what Louis referred to. Cordelia. And the real reason they'd been in London.

"We can't hide what we did, and why we're really here, from her forever," said Louis. "Accepting werewolves exist is a far bigger challenge, don't you think?"

Louis could tell himself that if it made him feel better, but Pierre couldn't shy away from the truth. "We stalked her online, uploaded malware to her computer, tracked her to London and then lied to her about being nothing more than her new neighbors. Oh, and the woman she believes is a victim, is really an evil witch with a vendetta against our pack. If finding out we're werewolves doesn't make her run, that will." He crossed his arms and leaned against the counter. "Or maybe you're referring to the fact she's our mate, and we want to claim her by biting her and turning into a one of us. After today, any mention of our teeth anywhere near her and she'll be on the next flight back to London."

Louis paled. "Maybe we wait a bit to tell her that part. Until she's not so afraid of us. But the rest of it... If not now, then when? The longer we leave it, the worse it'll be when it comes out."

Pierre would rather Melinda never found out, but Louis was right about one thing. They *would* have to tell her. If only for her own safety. Melinda continuing to believe Cordelia needed saving could be dangerous for them all.

A light footfall at the top of the stairs had them both freezing.

"Leaving?" whispered Louis.

"Where would she go?" he mouthed back.

The creak of the stairs continued as Melinda descended, heading not for the front door, but toward them. A little of the tightness eased in his chest. He hadn't been too certain she *wouldn't* leave.

Pierre set the kettle to boil as Melinda appeared in the doorway, uncertainty pouring off her. She eyed the teapot and the tin of jasmine tea laid out on the bench.

"I thought you might like some tea," he said.

She took a deep breath and blew it out again, her gaze flicking between them. He didn't dare move an inch, lest she bolt.

She stepped into the kitchen. "Do you know how to make it?" She cleared her throat. "Properly?"

He did. He'd watched her enough times on her security feed, longing to take her in his arms and soothe away her stress. Guilt lodged like a lump in his chest. "No." The lie tasted thick on his tongue. "Can you show me?"

She hesitated for a brief second, then joined him behind the kitchen counter. "You have cups?"

Louis produced three cups and set them on the counter.

"My mother taught me Gongfu Cha — the traditional way of making tea. It was important to her. Respecting tradition. She used to say it's a way of mindfulness and a way to connect with others, but also to yourself." She cradled the teapot. "This was my mother's."

"You were close?"

Melinda rubbed her hands over the pot with a reverence reserved for holy relics. "When it was the two of us, making tea, it was like the rest of the world didn't exist. We were in this bubble and nothing could touch us." Melinda set the pot on the counter. "That was most likely because my mother never made tea when my father was around."

That she was willing to share something of herself, of her past, those precious moments with her mother, touched him and buried him in a good measure of shame. What would she think of him — of them — when she found out what they'd done? What they were still doing? Maybe Louis was right. Maybe they should lay bare everything.

"Anyway, you have to warm the clay first." Melinda poured boiling water into the clay teapot and all three cups. "It helps prevent the pot from cracking, and it maintains the temperature so you get full flavor from the leaves." Her expression softened as she swished the water around before tipping it into the sink.

Pierre held up a cup. "These, too?"

She nodded, and he repeated swishing the water around in all three cups before discarding it.

From the tin, she scooped two large spoonfuls of fragrant leaves into the pot and raised it to her nose. She took a deep breath and smiled. "Jasmine. It was my mother's favorite. Every time I make it, every time I smell it, it's like she's still with me. Still here."

Pierre would buy her jasmine tea every day — hell, he'd buy the damn company — to see that expression on her face again and again.

Melinda ran the tap until she liked the temperature, then covered the leaves with water. "You don't want to shock the leaves by hitting them with boiling water," she said, the wistfulness gone from her voice. "This way, you release their full flavor by gradually exposing them to heat. It stops the tea from tasting bitter. See." She pointed into the pot, and they both leaned forward to peer in. "The leaves are unfurling."

That she didn't back away with them both so close, Pierre counted as a win. A step in the right direction.

"Then you rotate the pot to aid the infusion." She gently turned the pot twice. "Now we can add the boiling water."

As she talked, as the tea steeped, the subtle hint of jasmine in the air, her shoulders loosened. He shared a look with his twin. It had been a good idea to make the tea.

She poured them each a cup. Pierre was more of a coffee person, but he would drink a cup of hydrochloric acid right now if it made her happy.

Cradling hers, she backed away, putting space between them, and leaned against the cupboards. The wariness was still in her eyes, but the horror was gone. She opened her mouth to speak, but sipped on her tea instead.

"Ask your questions, Melinda." They would answer them. To the best of their ability.

"Would you ever have told me?"

"Yes," they both replied in unison.

"But…you barely know me."

Louis chuckled. "*Chouquette*, I think we know you quite well."

Pierre scowled at him. He wanted to punch his twin right now. They *did* know her well. They knew almost everything about her. From their deep dive into her past and from the security feeds. Hell, they knew what brand of toothpaste she used.

"Are you forgetting that time in Pierre's bedroom?" Louis ran his gaze down her body, mischief sparkling in his eyes. "Or on the plane?"

A pretty flush spread across her neck and cheeks. She frowned into her cup of tea. "Why would your brother say you would have died for me today?" She pinned him with her stare.

Putain. Right to the heart of things. Their little cipher mate was smart. And bold. He liked it, but was she ready to hear she was their mate?

Pierre set his cup on the counter and moved toward her. She stiffened, but didn't run. "Melinda," he said, shaking his head a little. "You feel this *passion* between us, *non?*"

Her breath hitched a little and her heart beat a little faster, but not from fear.

"More than *passion.*" He sidled closer, dropping his voice. "A connection." He reached out, taking the cup from her hands, setting it aside and placing her palm on his chest. "We feel it, too. And we want to explore it, as far as it will take us."

Louis skirted the counter, and they crowded her against the bench.

His twin ran a gentle hand down her cheek. "We're werewolves, Melinda. That's who we are."

Pierre nuzzled her neck, and she dropped her head back, granting him better access. "And if we're going to go all the way with this, you'd need to know."

"All the way," reiterated Louis.

Her body softened. "All the way," she whispered.

He slipped her hands around his neck, cupped her ass, and she wrapped her legs around his hips. "*Oui.*"

Louis pressed against her from behind.

She shivered, her thighs clenching against his hips. "*Oui.*"

His wolf wanted to howl his triumph. It prowled in his mind, urging him to bite, mark, claim and turn her. Now. *Non.* He forced it down. They must tread softly. Tonight was for gentleness, wooing, worshiping. Easing her fears. Not the rough, urgent rutting of a turning.

They would show her what she meant to them. Everything. What they could give her. All of them. A devotion unparalleled and unending until death claimed them. They would show her the benefit of their wolf senses. How they could scent her every desire, read her body's subtlest signals and give her what she wanted, what she needed. They would leave her satiated beyond her wildest dreams and in no doubt of how much she meant to them.

"The bedroom?" suggested Louis.

Melinda whimpered in his arms and rolled her hips, her hot little core pressing against his impatient cock.

He swung her around and sat her on the island bench. "*Non*. Here." He wasn't capable of more. Words failed him.

Louis growled and rushed to clear the counter of cups and Melinda's precious teapot. Pierre laid her across the cool surface and ran his hand down her throat, across her chest and down to the button of her jeans. She moaned, arching her back, the hard bead of her nipples poking through the fabric of her sweater.

Louis stood across the bench from him, at Melinda's head, his nostrils flaring. His twin's gaze met his. They needed no words.

She was beautiful, perfect, and they were going to show her what it meant to be theirs.

Melinda wasn't sure what she was doing. Why she was letting them touch her, but... Louis brushed her hair from her face, his lips a mere breath away from hers, the need reflected in his hazel eyes matching the fire coursing through her body. Pierre gripped her hips, firm but not painful. They would never hurt her. Had never hurt her. And, oh God, she wanted this. Wanted them. To take things *all the way*.

She parted her lips on a sigh, and Louis dove in as Pierre rolled his hips. Gentle hands tugged at the hem of her sweater. Another pair popped the button on her jeans and worked the zipper down. Then Louis' mouth was gone, and he guided her sweater over her head as Pierre tugged her jeans off.

"Putain."

The word exploded from Pierre's mouth, his Adam's apple jerking as he swallowed.

"You packed her sexy lingerie, Pierre?" Louis' eyes blazed. "I like it."

A low growl rumbled in Louis' throat, and wetness coated her panties. She should be afraid of this obvious manifestation of his wolf, but, God help her, it only turned her on more.

Louis ran his fingers beneath the strap of her bra. "But it has to go."

Yes.

"First, though…"

He leaned down, taking her nipple in his mouth, sucking it through the red lace. She all but bowed off the kitchen counter when Pierre did the same with her other nipple.

Oh, Lordy.

Her skin was flushed, her nipples were tight, and she reveled in their attention. Like with everything, the differences between Pierre and Louis were stark. Louis rolled his tongue around her nipple, plumping her breast, sucking deep, then backing off, a caress of his hot breath over her skin. No rhyme nor rhythm, whatever took his fancy. Pierre worked her with controlled strokes, molding her breast where he wanted it, the laving of his tongue interspersed with little nips, the faintest bite of pain, to her nipple, to the underside of her breast. The scratch of lace against her sensitized skin heightened the sensation.

Then Pierre lifted her up, and Louis flipped the clasp of her bra. The cold marble of the countertop as Pierre laid her back down did nothing to cool her heated skin. There was something more intimate about their tongues, their mouths, their hands on her bare flesh that had Melinda gasping for breath, her body putty in their hands and her heart... She let the thought slip away, snaking her fingers into their hair and tugging them closer.

Louis chuckled. "She likes this."

Pierre dropped a kiss beneath her breast, another at the top of her ribcage. His tongue flicked into her belly button and her stomach quivered. "She's going to like this even more."

He dropped another kiss below her belly button as he tore away her panties. Large hands settled on her thighs, pushing them wider, exposing her. Louis grasped her hands, wrapping her arms around his neck. Cool air teased her wet nipples as Pierre's hot breath brushed across her core. Nothing she'd ever experienced with a man had ever felt as right as being here, like this, with both of them.

Pierre ran his nose along her slit, breathing her in, a low rumble starting in his chest. "Divine," he murmured, then he replaced his nose with his tongue.

Laid out between them like this on the countertop, like a dinner for two, they devoured her. Louis, playful, teasing, his tongue dancing with hers, his hands exploring her body, never still. Pierre, determined, purposeful, swiping his tongue along her seam, before diving in, strong strokes in and out. With one hand on her thigh he kept her firmly in place, the other on her mound, his thumb an insistent press against her swollen clit. Melinda squirmed beneath their attentions. It was almost too much, too intense. She clasped at the collar of Pierre's shirt, her other hand in Louis' hair, and held on. Her body, charged as though she'd plugged herself into a live socket, floated on the edge of ecstasy.

Then Pierre changed the rhythm of his tongue, of his thumb, and her orgasm stuttered and stalled. *No.* She whimpered into Louis' mouth.

Louis grinned against her mouth. "Pierre, you *connard.* Are you playing with our little cipher?"

Pierre rumbled an assent that almost, *almost,* sent her over the edge, but then he withdrew from her, leaving her wet and needy and desperate.

Her chest heaving, she managed to get out one word, a mere whimper. "Pierre."

He nipped at her inner thigh, each tiny sting buzzing her clit. "Patience."

Melinda squirmed in their hold. She couldn't be patient. She needed release. *Now.*

"Trust me, Melinda. It will be worth the wait. I promise." Pierre muttered some analogy about coding, but Melinda was too far gone to make any sense of it.

"Please."

But Pierre ignored her begging.

"Louis?"

She chased after Louis' mouth. He gave it to her, and she sucked on his tongue as though it might take her over the edge.

He retreated, and she stared into his eyes, dark shadows shifting in their depths.

"If it was up to me, *mon amour, I* would give you what you need. You beg so beautifully, and I could not resist you. But" — he brushed his thumb over her lips, and she followed it with her tongue, tasting the saltiness of his skin—"Pierre is Pierre, and he would make you wait. Make us both wait."

He silenced her protests with his mouth. His fingers tweaked her aching nipple, rolling, rubbing as Pierre continued his silent, steady assault between her thighs, licking, sucking, avoiding both her clit and her G-spot on *purpose*, dragging her closer and closer to the edge again and again, never quite tipping her over.

Her body bathed in sweat, her hair plastered to her forehead, she was a quivering, needy mess when Pierre finally, *finally*, sucked her swollen, buzzing clit into his hot mouth.

Melinda exploded, white-hot pleasure ripping through her body. Her hands tightened around Louis' neck, her thighs capturing Pierre's head between them. They made no effort to free themselves, holding her firmly in place as spasm after spasm ripped through her. A nip at her clit, at her lip—the twins in sync in a way that seemed humanly impossible—sent her into a second orgasm, before she'd come down from the first. Her body spiraled, her mind consumed by the two of them—their mouths, their strong hands. Her head thrown back, she was incapable of sound or breath as wave after wave of pleasure rolled through her. Time stopped, and she hung suspended in the grip of sensation so intense she thought she might never come down again.

Her breathing labored, she flopped like a rag doll on the counter.

"See what we can do for you, *chouquette*," murmured Louis in her ear, sending residual shivers through her body. "And this is just the beginning."

The beginning? She didn't think she could cope with more, her body limp, basking in her afterglow. Her racing heart slowed and she rediscovered her ability to breathe. Cognizant thoughts returned, and Melinda realized she *did* want more. Not orgasms — though she wouldn't say no to that — but more of them. Apart from a hand in Pierre's hair, and a grip of Louis' collar, *she'd* not touched *them.* They'd given her the best orgasms of her life, laid her out naked and worshiped her body, and they'd not removed a stitch of their clothing. It'd all been about her.

She wanted it to be about them, too. She craved a closeness and an intimacy that could only come when all of them were equally invested. On the jet, she'd been so eclipsed by her fear and her need to forget, she'd barely been aware. A willing participant, taking from them what she needed. As with now, it had all been about her needs. It was time for it to be about *them.* What *they* needed.

Chapter Twenty-Two

Pierre released his grip on Melinda's thighs as she struggled to rise. The uncertainty in Louis' eyes matched the sensation swirling in his gut. Would she retreat from them again now? Like she had on the plane? He backed away, letting her slip down from the counter. He'd never be able to come into this kitchen, make tea, or sit here and eat again without thinking of this night. Of her splayed between them, writhing and moaning as they worked her body to a crescendo. He did not want this to be the end, or their last time touching their mate, but as she headed for the door, he feared it might be.

She paused in the doorway, naked, beautiful, her skin flushed. She glanced over her shoulder at them and tipped her head toward the stairs, a hesitant vulnerability in her eyes. He shared a glance with Louis. She was asking them for something, but what?

They followed her up the stairs, his balls so tight and his cock so hard each step was a pain all of its own. He would have walked through hellfire for Melinda if she'd asked him to.

In the main suite, she paused beside the bed. Another look shared with his twin. This wasn't goodbye. She wanted them. *Thank fuck.* They surged toward her, but she held her palms out, stopping them in their tracks.

"Twice now, you've given me what *I* needed." There was a tremor in her voice, and a stutter in her heartbeat as her gaze bounced between the two of them. "Now I'm going to give you what you need."

What they needed? Their needs were simple. Her.

She placed a palm on his chest, his body responding in an instant, ready and willing. His wolf pushed forward.

Her fingers rubbed against his chest, almost petting him, soothing him. "Pierre, you like to watch, yes?"

Pierre. Not Louis. Not you. His heart beat a loud drum in his chest. "*Oui.*"

Her tremulous smile almost stole away the remnants of his control.

Her attention fixed on him, she took Louis' hand. "Then watch."

She turned Louis toward the bed, pushing him so he sat on the edge. Louis went willingly, if somewhat confused. He reached for her, but she took his hands and placed them beside his hips.

"I've had my turn. Now it's yours."

Before he could protest, she cupped his face and slanted her mouth over his. Louis took her offering, keeping his hands where she'd put them as Pierre palmed himself through his jeans, rooted to the spot. She broke the kiss, guiding Louis' shirt up over his head.

She gasped, small hands fluttering over his brother's chest to his shoulder, to the puckered pink scar. "This was where you were shot?"

Louis shrugged. "It's almost healed."

Sad eyes found his. "And you too, Pierre?"

He'd all but forgotten a bullet had gone through his thigh. By tomorrow, it would be nothing more than a memory. "I'd take a hail of bullets for you, Melinda. We both would." And it was the truth.

She leaned in and kissed Louis' scar, her attention fixed on him, and *putain*, didn't the bullet wound in his thigh burn as if it was his injury she was kissing. Over his brother's chest, she forged a trail of kisses. Pierre moved in for a better angle. She flicked her pink tongue out, laving his twin's nipple. Watching her with Louis was like watching himself with her in the mirror. His own nipple was on fire, as though she'd touched him. Licked him. Blunt human teeth clamped around the taut bud, and both he and Louis moaned.

"Melinda, you don't have to—"

She cut Louis off with a finger to his lips. "I want to."

Louis' shocked gaze found his. Melinda wanted to seduce *them*? A slow grin spread across his face. The fates had chosen their mate well.

Melinda pushed Louis back onto the bed, her fingers working at the button and zipper of his jeans. She dragged them off, with a willing hand from Louis, and tossed them aside. His boxer briefs followed.

"You too, Pierre."

Oui. He toed off his boots and had his shirt off and his jeans around his ankles before she could blink. He kicked them aside, enraptured.

She gripped his brother's swollen cock. Louis' stomach muscles bunched, and Pierre's own cock throbbed, a bead of pre-cum glistening on the end.

With her gaze on him, she licked Louis' length from base to tip. The urge to take himself in hand made him tremble, and when she took Louis in her mouth, it took every ounce of control he had to stop himself.

It wasn't his hand he wanted, it was hers. Her hand, her mouth, her *minou*. Anything else would be a poor substitute. So he stood there, rooted to the spot, his nails digging into his palms, and watched as Louis reveled in her attentions, his twin's eyes closed and his hands fisted in the duvet.

It was the most erotic thing he'd ever seen in his life. Their mate on her knees, her arousal thick in the air, her dark gaze locked with his as she pleasured his twin. The intimacy of it, the generosity. Pierre had never been so close to the edge. The connection sizzled in the air between them, but it was more than that. She saw them. Him and Louis. Recognized their differences. Their needs. She understood his need to relish in the sweet torture of watching her with his brother. The build up, the test of his control over his own body. And she accepted that. Accepted him. Wolf shifter and all. What a precious gift. He would give her the world right now if she asked it of him.

"Melinda, I'm going to—" Louis stiffened, and a guttural groan ripped from his mouth. He abandoned the duvet for her hair, tangling his fingers in the silky black strands, holding her still as he roared his release. He collapsed back on the bed, his skin flushed and his chest heaving.

Louis, still catching his breath, heaved himself up and Melinda with him. She squealed, clutching at his shoulders.

"*Mon amour*"—Louis took her mouth in his, kissing her deep, before releasing her lips—"Pierre has had enough of watching."

Fuck, yes.

His brother handed Melinda to him, and she wrapped her legs around his hips, grinding his erection between them. *Merde.* She was ready. More than ready. Slick with her need. He was not going to keep her wanting. Not after what she'd done for them tonight.

"Wait." Concern rippled across Melinda's face. "What about condoms? I know shifters can't carry diseases, but…"

Putain. There would come a day when wearing protection to ease Melinda's very human concerns would no longer be necessary. When they'd had the conversation, spelling out for her exactly who she was to them, her claiming, her turning. How he would love to put a pup in her womb, once she was one of them. That until then there was no possibility of either of them getting her pregnant. But he didn't think Melinda was ready to hear about fated mates. Or them biting her. And right now, talking wasn't what he wanted to be doing.

Louis pressed a condom into Melinda's hand. His twin was of the same mind as he was. Pierre sat on the edge of the bed, balancing her on his knees as she rolled the prophylactic over his length. No more waiting. He lifted her up and lowered her onto his shaft.

For a moment, he lost all ability to breathe. Her head dropped back and her mouth parted on a silent gasp. Louis closed in behind her, palming her breast and devouring her mouth, and Pierre rolled his hips. Slow, steady, with each stroke telling her what she meant to him. What she would always mean to him. He would spend the rest of his life showing her, making sure she never had cause to doubt it.

* * * *

The sensation of being watched had Louis opening one eye. Nestled between him and Pierre, the covers tousled around her legs, lay Melinda. Her breathing even, she didn't stir. His brother, his body wrapped around their mate, a protective cocoon against the dangers of the outside world, slept on. If not Pierre or Melinda, what had awoken him?

He sensed no threat, but with Cordelia out there somewhere, free to wreak havoc with some very powerful magic, Louis wasn't going to ignore the sensation.

He blinked, scanning the darkened room before settling on two eyes, a greenish glow to their amber depths, staring at him from a furry face. Melinda's cat.

Manchu had paused on the end of the bed, one foot suspended in the air mid stride, his eyes narrowed on him. Louis pushed his wolf down, resisting the urge to respond to the animal's aggression. Melinda cared for Manchu. Louis cared for Melinda.

More than cared. She was everything he'd ever hoped for, and more. She'd astounded him tonight. Bowled him over with each light touch of her hands, each press of her mouth on his body.

She'd given them far more than pleasure. She'd seen them. Him *and* Pierre. Acknowledged their different needs. Catered to them. They'd waited for her, searched for her for years. A pint-sized ginger furball was *not* going to get in their way. Somehow, they would have to make peace with it.

Though his wolf protested at any show of submission, Louis dropped his gaze, breaking the standoff between them. Every sense attuned to the tiny animal, he followed Manchu's slow progress up Melinda's leg, one hesitant paw after another. The cat crested Melinda's hip and paused again. Louis risked a peek. Amber eyes regarded him, accompanied by a furious swish of a ginger tail and a hiss.

Louis kept his breathing steady and his body still, avoiding eye contact. His wolf wanted nothing more than to put this impudent feline in its place, show it who was the dominant animal, but that would achieve nothing except reinforce the cat's fear of them.

Manchu continued his journey up Melinda's body, dipping at her waist, then climbing up her arm and onto her shoulder. There, he settled, wrapping his tail around his little body and tucking his paws beneath his chest. Sitting there between him and Pierre, guarding Melinda. *Brave little fucker. Loyal, too.*

Keeping his movements smooth and slow, Louis reached for the bag of fishy cat treats he'd stashed in the bedside drawer. He held one out to Manchu.

Suspicion flickered in those amber eyes. Louis kept his hand steady, and stretched a little closer to the ginger furball. Manchu sniffed the air.

"That's a good boy. Take the treat. It's tasty." Louis wouldn't eat it, but he hoped it would appeal to a cat.

"What are you trying to do, Louis?"

He should've known his brother would be awake, too. Nothing much got past a wolf. "Tempting Manchu with food."

"Just because the way to your heart is through your stomach doesn't mean that approach will work with the cat."

"No," Louis conceded. "But the way to Melinda's heart is through Manchu. Have you got a better idea?"

Manchu extended a paw, then retreated. Louis held his breath. Manchu made another pass, this time snagging Louis' hand, drawing it closer, until he could snatch the treat.

Louis lay back down next to Melinda. Manchu eyed him with slitted eyes, but Louis caught the subtle rumble of a purr.

Louis closed his eyes. In this moment, he could believe all was right in their world. It wasn't, but that was a worry for tomorrow, and morning would come soon enough. Cordelia was still out there. Their deception yet to be revealed. When it was, when everything came to light, Louis worried it could destroy everything.

Chapter Twenty-Three

The San Francisco Bay came into focus as the vision left her, and Cordelia hid her satisfaction by sipping her tea. If the Langeais wolves thought sending her grimoire to the wolf witch, Alain d'Louncrais, would stop her from coming for it, they were sadly mistaken. She would storm the Bastille in the eighteenth century to get it back if she had to.

Whitecaps dotted the water, and dark clouds loomed on the horizon. A storm was coming, and the Langeais wolves would bear the brunt of it. As would the Bayside coven. Less than a block away was the home of Marjory Jackson, former High Priestess. Cordelia smirked. She was right under their noses and they had no idea. Not in some abandoned warehouse down by the docks. Or some rundown cabin in the woods. No more mud huts, peasant villages, or poverty for her. Not anymore.

Cordelia turned from the window, her gaze lighting on the two men in her parlor. Dutton, her grandson — though still recovering from the stab wounds inflicted by Annabelle, he could yet be of use—and Regis Veilleux, the vaunted leader of the Faucherians. She suppressed a snort. If the man had any brains, he would change the damn name of his organization. But his hatred, and subsequently his people's hatred, of the Langeais wolves made for good, expendable foot soldiers.

He'd first sent her Gerard Boucher, but with Gerard dead at the hands of Gabriel Montagne, Veilluex had come in person. Boucher had been little more than a thug. In Veilleux's eyes glimmered keen intelligence with a side serving of cunning. He was the true mastermind behind the rise of the Faucherians. Rumor had it he had connections in some very high places. Connections that could prove useful to her. Or they could turn on her at a moment's notice.

She'd played the long game for decades. Across centuries. She had patience and money and power. At her age, what she no longer had was time. Despite the deep well of magic at her fingertips, even she couldn't stop the inevitable. Death would claim her like everyone else. At eighty-five, her days were numbered. The return of her grimoire, and the spells within it, would help her stave it off a little longer.

Her gaze narrowed on the Frenchman. "Your men were a little too enthusiastic in their charade, Veilleux. I have bruises on my arms."

Vielleux snarled. "Six of my men are dead. Where were *your* powers when zey were dying?" Veilleux's French accent was not normally as pronounced, but in his anger it thickened. "Zink yourself lucky all you 'ave are bruises. Do we even want ze same zing, *Cordelia*? Mm?" He said her name as though he'd tasted something foul on his tongue.

Her wrinkled, age-spotted hands gripped her tea cup. She wouldn't tolerate being spoken to like a mere human. She could turn him into the very thing he hated. That which he hunted. The thought had some appeal. She doubted Veilluex would have the fortitude to master the beast within as *he* had.

She breathed through the temptation. Not yet. "I told you to send more men." She infused enough ice in her voice to freeze over San Francisco Bay.

Men never listened. It wasn't her problem if he'd paid the price. It *was* her problem those blasted twins still walked the earth. Them, and their brother, were thorns in her side. As was the hacker she'd used. The bleeding-heart crusader hellbent on saving her. She'd suited her purpose until the Montagne twins had tracked the stupid girl down. Blast her second sight for the lack of warning. On this, it had been silent.

"I underestimated the twins." A grudging admission from an arrogant man. "They're *pirate informatiques,* not soldiers."

Fool. They were werewolves first. Had he thought them weedy little men hunched over their desks, squinting at their computer screens? "Where are they now?"

"At the Ritz-Carlton."

"And the girl?"

"With zem. I 'ave men on it. Ze 'otel is crawling wiz shifters. Taking 'er from ze 'otel is too risky, but ze moment zey make a move, we'll know."

She turned to Dutton. "The others?"

"Annabelle and her mutt, Gabriel, have gone to ground with Isobella and the d'Louncrais she-wolf. They're still planning on using your spell to go back to the tenth century. From the whispers I'm hearing, it's Isobella going back in time, not Annabelle."

Isobella? No. That cannot *happen.*

Dutton helped himself to a whiskey from her sideboard. Annabelle choosing to mate a werewolf over him still consumed him. Dutton needed to find himself a willing bedmate. It was what she'd been forced to do all those years ago.

"It makes no sense to me," said Dutton, between sips of whiskey. "Isobella is unwell. No one's talking, but I tracked her to the hospital the other day. Cancer, I think. Why send *her* back?"

Because, you stupid sod, of what she becomes. Cordelia had seen it. The woman she knew as Isobella using *her* spell to journey back in time, and mating the other pair of Montagne twins, the tenth-century ones. She remembered them well. Big brutes of men. Pure Frankish blood. No hint of the bronzed skin of their descendants. "We can't allow Isobella to go back to the tenth century."

Dutton's glass halted part way to his lips. "Forgive me, Aunt Cordelia, but... It was you who suggested the coven send someone back to the tenth century. Now you want us to stop it?"

With Annabelle under their control, sending *her* back to the tenth century had been a masterful plan. Two-fold in nature. She was an unknown, and unexpected. A lost and helpless female, the d'Louncrais would've taken her in. As they'd taken in Cordelia when she'd arrived in the village, her belly rounded with a babe. Through her, they could have wreaked havoc on the Langeais wolves. On the d'Louncrais. And Annabelle wasn't Isobella. Preventing Isobella from going back in time would strike a blow close to the heart of the Langeais wolves. All three Montagnes—Gabriel, Pierre and Louis—would cease to exist. And it would do much more than that. She could not let Isobella succeed.

But no matter how much she tried, Cordelia had yet to subvert fate. What use were her damn visions if she couldn't use them to alter the course of history?

"You don't have to understand," she snapped.

Dutton dropped his gaze. "Of course. I'll update Douglas. He'll see it done."

"I'll allocate a few of my operatives to assist him," said Veilleux.

The man might not have an ounce of esoteric power running through his veins, but where Dutton had failed to make the connection, Veilleux hadn't. She would have to keep a close watch on the leader of the Faucherians. He would turn on her. Eventually. When he did, she'd be ready for him. And she wouldn't make the mistake of turning him into a werewolf. Not like she had all those centuries ago with *him*. When he'd rejected her.

Him. Alexandre d'Louncrais. Her creation. The first ever Langeais wolf. It had all started with him. And here, in the twenty-first century, his ancestors continued to flourish. Progeny begotten from the womb of that wretched nobleman's daughter, Genevieve. Alexandre was long dead, lost to dust over the centuries, but it was not enough to ease the rage that burned in her chest.

"Dutton, fetch me that country bumpkin herbalist, Grace Williams. I have a task for her. Call her mother in, too." A little leverage went a long way. She pinned the Faucherian leader with her gaze. "And Veilluex, get me that hacker."

She'd wipe out the Montagnes, get rid of anyone who could trace her, and Grace would get her back her grimoire. Then she would finish off the d'Louncrais and the rest of the Langeais wolves once and for all. She'd created them. She was going to destroy them.

Chapter Twenty-Four

Melinda, with Manchu snuggled on her lap, closed another tab, resisting the urge to shove her laptop clear across the table. *Nothing.* It'd been four days since the events at the abandoned warehouse and neither she nor the twins had found any trace of MysticMage. Four days hunched over her laptop. Four nights spent in a super-sized king bed lapping up the attentions of two insatiable men. Werewolves. Their stamina far surpassed hers. In the wee hours of the morning, thoroughly sated, she would succumb to a deep and dreamless sleep.

Today, guilt was riding her hard. How could she lose herself to passion, how could she sleep so undisturbed when her poor client was...? It didn't bear thinking about.

Across the table from her, surrounded by tech Melinda would've given a kidney for, Louis devoured a large slice of pecan pie with whipped cream. Yesterday, it'd been apple pie. The day before, banana cream. American pastries leaned more to the pie variety, and Louis seemed determined to try them all.

Pierre pushed back from his chair. "I'm going to make more coffee. Anyone want any? Melinda, tea?"

A chorus of yes, pleases, and Melinda leaned back in her chair, her gaze glued to Pierre's taut ass as he sauntered into the kitchen.

Louis chuckled. "Can't wait until tonight, *bébé?*"

Melinda flushed and glared at her lover. They weren't the only ones in the room. Gabriel, phone to his ear, paced to a backdrop of blue sky and city buildings. Stefanie and Annabelle lounged on the sofa. All three were werewolves. If what she'd learned about Louis' and Pierre's enhanced senses was anything to go by, she might as well shout it from the rooftops she was having sex with both of them. But having intimate conversations in front of other people wasn't something she was used to, even if it was the norm for werewolves.

Annabelle wasn't just a werewolf. She was a witch, too. Not that Melinda had seen any evidence of that yet. Pierre had assured her it was true, and that Annabelle had played a role in the warehouse, keeping her safe and helping them. Melinda had been too busy hiding behind a barrel, terrified, to witness anything.

What did it even mean to be a witch? Boiling cauldrons, pointy hats and a big book of spells? Weird occult-like ceremonies in the forest? Annabelle, despite being both a werewolf and a witch, appeared completely normal.

Isobella, Annabelle's sister, was a witch, too. A sick one. She wasn't here today. She'd had an appointment with her oncologist. Witchcraft, it seemed, had its limitations.

Pierre returned as Gabriel finished his call.

Stefanie accepted a coffee from Pierre. "What did my big brother have to say?"

"He's sent back up. They should be here tonight."

"Good." Annabelle sipped her coffee. "I don't think we can wait much longer. Isobella's oncologist is pushing her to start some form of treatment. If she has surgery or chemo, or both as he's suggesting, she'll be too sick, too weak to go. We can't hold off any longer."

"Wait for what? Go where?" Melinda smiled her thanks to Pierre for her tea.

It hadn't escaped her notice that although Annabelle, Stef, Pierre and Louis had filled her in on werewolves, there were still things they weren't telling her. Things everyone in the room except her knew. She could understand why they'd kept secret their true identity. It wasn't something one bought up in casual conversation. But now she knew, why would they continue to keep secrets from her? Hadn't they said she'd get *all* of them?

Louis and Pierre looked to Gabriel, and after a pause, the big man nodded.

Pierre pulled up a chair beside her. "Melinda, Isobella is taking a trip back in time to the tenth century."

Melinda almost choked on her tea. "You're kidding me, right?" *Time travel? Really?*

"No, Melinda, he's not joking," said Annabelle, swiveling around to face her. "We have a spell to transport a person through time." She grimaced. "It's not pleasant, but it works. I know. I've tried it."

Gabriel grunted. Perhaps he'd tried it, too. Or maybe it was an expression of the protectiveness he seemed to have for his mate. Annabelle didn't seem to mind.

Melinda wouldn't mind it either, if it came from Pierre and Louis.

Melinda set her tea down on the table. "Okay. I'll bite. *Why* is Isobella going back in time? And why to the tenth century?" If they were open to talking, Melinda wasn't going to waste this chance, no matter how ridiculous it seemed. After all, werewolves existed. And so did witches. Why not time travel. "Are you hunting a powerful relic or something?"

"No." Pierre shifted in his chair. "It's a bit more complicated than that."

The stillness in the room unnerved her. Whatever it was, it was big.

"Isobella is our many times great grandmother," Louis blurted out.

Pierre glared at his twin.

Louis held up his hands. "What? There's no point dancing around the subject. Like a sticking plaster, you just rip that sucker off."

Their many times great grandmother? Her gaze skipped from one set of earnest eyes to the next, then back to Louis and Pierre. They were serious. "Does Isobella know about this?"

"About going back in time? Yes." Annabelle rose from the sofa and skirted the table. "That she will mate these guys' ancestors? No."

At Annabelle's closeness, Manchu leaped from her lap and flew up the stairs. Pierre and Louis he tolerated—Louis mostly because he fed Manchu treats at every opportunity—but he didn't like any of the others getting near him.

"So, let me get this straight. You're sending a sick woman back in time, with a spell that—in your own words — is unpleasant. Then she's going to have to mate with some tenth-century barbarian?"

Annabelle held up two fingers. "Two barbarians, actually. Twins run in the family."

Melinda gaped at Annabelle. "And you're okay with this? I mean, Isobella's your sister. I don't know a damn thing about the tenth century, but I'm pretty sure they don't have oncologists and chemotherapy there. Do they even have hospitals?" Melinda took in the room, the unconcerned faces looking at her. "You're sending her there to die. After…after…"

Gabriel cuffed Louis across the back of the head. "You idiots. You've told her nothing."

Pierre snarled at Gabriel. "Like you told Annabelle?"

What was she missing here? Something important. Perhaps profound. She rubbed her chest, attempting to ease the tightness. Instinct, and the way Pierre and Louis couldn't meet her eyes, told her it somehow concerned her. Maybe Manchu had the right idea, but she remained in her seat. She had to know. "Told me what?"

Pierre reached for her hands, but she tucked them against her chest.

"Told me what?"

Pierre's hazel eyes pleaded with her to understand. "There are certain things about us we can only reveal in…certain situations."

Gabriel rolled his eyes. "Have you three talked at all in the last few days?"

This time, both Louis and Pierre snarled.

"Cut us some slack, Gabriel. She's only known werewolves exist for four days. It's a lot to take in." Louis rounded the table and joined his twin, blocking the others from view. He pulled out a chair and dropped into it, leaning in close. "There are other werewolf clans besides ours, but the Langeais wolves are different from them."

Langeais? Is that somewhere in France?

"We are the only true werewolf pack."

True werewolf pack? What the hell does that mean?

"Unless you count the Ludenwic wolves in London and the Rus wolves in Russia," added Gabriel.

Pierre bared his fangs at his brother. "You're not helping right now."

He turned back to Melinda, his canines sliding back up into his gums, and Melinda fought the urge to shrink away from him, from those teeth. This was *Pierre*.

"Us"—Pierre sent a loaded glare in his brother's direction—"the Ludenwic wolves and the Rus wolves are the only werewolves who can…turn human beings into werewolves."

Oh, God. Melinda was out of her chair, retreating. Annabelle, Stefanie and Isobella had never mentioned *that* when they'd had their talk in the bar downstairs. Because she'd not asked that question? She hadn't known enough to ask it.

Annabelle shrugged. "Sorry, Melinda." The witch's face beamed with sincerity. "It's not knowledge the pack sanctions to be spread. It wasn't our place to tell you."

She could understand why. Werewolves running around, turning humans into more werewolves—it was like something out of a black-and-white horror film. Her eyes widened. Did they do that? Would Pierre and Louis do that?

Pierre stiffened, his expression shuttered. "We don't do that, Melinda."

What? How did he…?

Hurt flashed in Louis' eyes. "We can read your body, your scent, *chouquette.* You were imagining us roaming the streets of San Francisco looking for fresh victims. That's not how things work."

No? How did they work then?

"Our alpha must sanction all turnings," explained Pierre. "It's been that way for centuries. There's only ever been one reason he'll accept a turning without question."

"And that reason is?"

The entire room held its breath as every gaze settled on her.

Chapter Twenty-Five

Louis hadn't wanted Melinda to find out like this. Tension held his twin's body rigid. Neither had Pierre. It was all kinds of fucked up. A room full of people. Everyone staring at her. Melinda the only human.

Stefanie rose from the sofa and grabbed her purse. "I think this might be our cue to leave. Give these guys some time to talk, hm?"

Melinda sucked in a breath. Did she not want to be alone with them now? He could only hope, as with the night she'd found out they were werewolves, Melinda would come around. That the developing bond between the three of them would be too strong for her to resist and would override her fear.

The click of the door closing behind the others was loud in the silence of the penthouse.

"Don't be afraid of us, Melinda. Please." He reached for her, but she took another step back. "Have we not proved ourselves to you over the last few days?"

Her distrust tainting the air, Melinda clenched and unclenched her hands. Louis couldn't blame her. It must seem as though she was being hit with one secret after another. The most damaging one was yet to come. If Pierre had his way, it would never come out.

She wiped her hands down her jeans. *Merde.* He wanted to scoop her up in his arms and comfort her, promise her the world. He'd give it to her, too. So would Pierre. But she wasn't having any of that right now, and if he made any move, he suspected she'd run.

Melinda raised her chin. "Tell me what reason your alpha would accept without question."

Straight to the heart of it all. Courageous little thing. Fierce pride burned in his chest.

"First," said Pierre, "you must understand why."

"How about we all relax a little?" suggested Louis. Standing here, Melinda looking like at any moment she might decide this was all too much for her, and Pierre — as rigid as a marble statue, the muscle ticking in his jaw the only hint he wasn't — wasn't helping anything. "Melinda, why don't you go make yourself comfortable on the sofa? Pierre will make you some more tea, and I'll order us some room service. Something sweet. How about some key lime pie? It was the next one on my list to try."

"Really, Louis?" Pierre snapped. "We're in the middle of something important here. And you've just *had* a huge slice of pecan pie not five minutes ago. Now is not the time to indulge ourselves."

Louis begged to differ. Now was the perfect time for a little comfort food. "Pierre." He turned to his brother, allowing a hint of fang to show. "Go make Melinda some tea."

Pierre opened his mouth to protest further. Louis growled, a low rumble deep in his chest, and he bared his teeth at his twin. It was rare for him to step up and give the orders. Pierre had always been the more dominant twin, always in charge. Louis had no need, or desire, to question the status quo, happy to follow his brother's lead. But sometimes his brother's desire to control things meant he missed the emotional signals. When things called for a gentler approach. Like now.

Pierre stormed off to the kitchen to make tea. Perhaps the ritual would do for Pierre what it did for Melinda. Louis dialed up the kitchen, gesturing for Melinda to find a comfortable spot on the sofa, and ordered three slices of pie with whipped cream.

By the time Pierre had steeped the tea, room service had arrived.

Louis handed Melinda a plate. "Key lime pie. Some say it's synonymous with the Florida Keys, but it gets its name from the key limes used to make it." At Melinda's raised eyebrows, he winked. "I did a little research." He always did. *Terroir* was important.

He thought he saw a hint of a smile. He'd take it.

Pierre joined them with tea for three, taking Louis' lead and sitting next to him, leaving Melinda alone on the sofa, the large glass coffee table an effective barrier between them. If giving Melinda space was what she needed, she would have it. The eye twitch and the clench of his jaw told Louis how much it cost Pierre.

Oui. It was a struggle for him, too. But when they were the ones she feared, crowding her wouldn't help their cause.

Louis scooped a forkful of pie and whipped cream into his mouth. What should be a delight, a balance of sweet and tart, tasted like ash. "Mm, this is good." He nudged Pierre. "You should try it."

Pierre stared at the pie as though Louis had served him up *escargot*. Give a werewolf bloody meat, brains or liver and he'll salivate. Slugs, not so much.

Pierre shoved a bite of pie into his mouth, chewed and swallowed. Then another, his expression never changing. It was torture watching him.

That hint of a smile was back on Melinda's lips. At Pierre's expense. He supposed it *was* a little funny — Pierre forcing himself to eat something he detested.

Melinda dug her fork into the pie and cream and took a tentative taste. "It's good."

Nothing like food to bring people together. He ate another forkful, then set his plate down. "Now, before we answer your question, Melinda, first there are a few things you should know about the Langeais wolves."

Melinda plonked her plate down and grabbed her tea like it was a lifeline. *Oui.* Maybe she was going to need it.

Pierre abandoned the plate of sweet pie and picked up his tea, too. Anything to wash away the combination of lime, cream and pastry. He didn't have the love of sweet things Louis did, but he had to give it to his twin. Melinda was not as close as he would've liked, but she was still here. In the penthouse. With them.

Louis jerked his head in Melinda's direction. "Tell her all about us, Pierre."

He shot his brother a filthy look. Typical. Louis was the lover, the charmer. He wouldn't back down from a fight, but he never liked to be the one to deliver unpleasant news or make a difficult decision. *That* he preferred to leave to Pierre.

He set his cup on the table, leaned forward, elbows on his knees, his hands clasped together save he reach for her. "The Langeais wolves are an ancient pack, and we have a few key differences to other shifter clans."

He paused. Melinda's white-knuckled grip on her cup made his chest tight and his wolf whine in his mind. *Putain.* He'd imagined having this conversation with her. In the afterglow of their lovemaking, Melinda cradled between them, all languid, soft and flushed. Not like this.

"As Annabelle and Stef would have told you, we're longer lived, impervious to disease and hard to kill."

Her gaze flicked from his thigh to Louis' shoulder. She'd witnessed how fast they healed.

"And now you know we can turn humans into werewolves."

She sipped her tea, trying to cover the little hitch in her breath. Nothing escaped them. She'd have to know that, too. If not from Annabelle and Stef, then from the four days they'd spent together.

"There's a reason for that." There was no good way to say this. Best to follow Louis' lead and dive right in. "Langeais wolves can't procreate with humans, and sometimes our fated mates aren't werewolves."

"Fated mates?"

That was the part she'd focused on? Fated mates? He shared a look with Louis. Perhaps there was hope for them yet.

Fated mates? Melinda's whole body lit up at the thought. *Why do I like the sound of that so much?* Then her brain kicked in and absorbed what Pierre had said. Langeais wolves can't procreate with humans, and sometimes their fated mates *aren't* werewolves. "Like Annabelle?"

"Exactly." Louis grinned and slapped a hand on Pierre's shoulder. "Our little cipher is smart."

Our little cipher? The words had her mind tumbling over everything she'd learned, everything she'd seen. The way Gabriel was with Annabelle. How he'd said Pierre and Louis would die for her. How Annabelle had said Isobella would mate not one, but two Montagne ancestors. *Twins.* Her mind raced to the pace of her furiously beating heart. Could that mean...? Melinda wasn't sure she was ready for the answer to that question.

"So, Isobella, when she mates your ancestors," she asked instead, "they'll turn her into a werewolf and that'll cure her cancer?"

"*Oui*, it will," affirmed Pierre.

"But she doesn't know she's going to mate a werewolf. Or two."

"No, but"—Louis shrugged—"she's probably figured out she's going to get turned into one. All the same, we can't tell her or we risk changing something."

Melinda sipped her tea, letting it all sink in. Her mind circled back to her unspoken question. To what the implications were for her. Would they risk telling her all this, revealing their true nature if she wasn't...? "Does it hurt?"

Louis dropped his head, and Pierre pushed himself back on the sofa, his expression shuttered. She focused on Pierre. If anyone was going to deliver the bad news, it would be him.

He cleared his throat. "The turning lasts for three days and is..." His Adam's apple bobbed in his throat. "Painful. *But* we have medication to temper the pain now. No one would suffer needlessly. We'd sedate them."

Them. No one. Abstract terms. Not her. Not you. Was this his way of telling her she wasn't their mate? She resisted the urge to rub at the burn in her chest. Did she want to be their mate? "And the bite?"

Louis raised his head and smirked. "We're focused on other things when it happens."

She gaped at them. "You do it when you're having *sex*?"

"*Oui,*" said the twins in unison, Louis openly grinning, Pierre determined.

The trill of a phone interrupted them.

"Ignore it," said Louis.

Pierre stared at his phone. "I can't. It's Maxime."

Louis face palmed. "He has the worst timing."

Pierre levered himself off the sofa. "It's our alpha, Melinda. I have to take this."

His phone to his ear, Pierre paced by the window, talking in low tones. Louis focused on his key lime pie. He wouldn't tell her anything more without Pierre. Was there anything more to tell? They'd said she'd have all of them, they'd called her theirs, but that didn't mean... She'd known them all of...what...two weeks? It seemed like a lifetime ago she'd suspected them of stalking her, only to discover they were her new neighbors. Two weeks wasn't enough time to develop anything serious. Was it? But Gabriel had said...

Pierre ended his call. "We have a new lead. Regis Veilleux is the leader of the men with the fancy F tattoos on their necks. Five days ago, he flew into San Francisco."

"Does Maxime have a photo?" asked Louis.

Pierre's phone dinged. "He sent it through."

Melinda set her tea down. "I guess we better get onto that, then. Find this man. Wherever he is, that's where my client will be."

Both Louis and Pierre looked pained.

Pierre pinned her with his gaze. "This conversation isn't over, but—"

"—we'll track down this Veilleux and find your client first," finished Louis.

Melinda nodded. "Okay. Let's get to work. I'll just…" She pointed at the stairs. "Too many cups of tea."

She dashed up the stairs, hyper-aware of twin gazes following her. Melinda had her own thoughts about finding her client, and perhaps this Veilleux guy.

The malware.

With everything that had happened in London—the break in, the assassin in her apartment, their desperate flight to San Francisco and the craziness that had happened since—she'd forgotten all about it. She'd once suspected Pierre and Louis were behind it.

After using the bathroom, she fished around for her purse and pulled out the USB drive. On it, a nasty little virus. If she could trace the malware, she might be able to get a location. Or at least a region. Then she'd let the virus do its work and shut down their tech. A little payback was in order.

The soft rumble of male voices filtered up the stairs. She popped the USB into her pocket and headed back down.

Pierre had set her key lime pie beside her laptop, and she ate a few more bites as she ran a thorough diagnostic check on her firewalls. Then she amped up her security, before opening up the identity she'd created. The one that had triggered the cyber-attack. Using every skill she had, she teased apart the malware, looking for weakness, for hints of who might have created it. It was an elegant piece of code. And she was going to use it against its owner. It'd been used to track her. If she could reverse it, turn it on itself...

There. Yes!

With the twins absorbed in their work, tapping away at their keyboards, she worked the code.

"You've been quiet for a while, Melinda." Louis set a fresh cup of tea in front of her.

"I'm working on something. I'm not sure if it's going to work, but...we'll see."

Pierre glanced at her over his screen. "Need any help?"

"I think I've sorted it. But if it doesn't work, I might take you up on that offer."

Both Louis and Pierre were brilliant. Working with them on something like this would be...amazing. But they had their hands full chasing down this Veilluex guy.

Melinda plugged the USB into her laptop. Accessing the file she needed, she attached the virus to the altered malware code, weaving it through in much the same way the hacker had weaved the malware through her IDS alerts.

"I've got him," said Louis, peering at his screen. "At the international terminal at San Francisco airport."

Pierre leaned over for a closer look. "He's not on any manifest. Must have used a fake passport."

Louis smirked. "Doesn't matter. Not when we have access to facial recognition tech."

Melinda double checked her firewalls and gave her code a final look over. If this worked, in a matter of minutes, she might have the information they needed.

Melinda hit enter and sent it through cyberspace.

Chapter Twenty-Six

Alarms blared from Pierre's computer. *No. It couldn't be.*

Pierre tapped furiously at his keyboard.

"Pierre?" Louis was out of his chair and standing behind his twin. "Veilleux? The Faucherians?"

Faucherians?

"No, it's—"

They both gaped at her over Pierre's screen. She'd not seen fear in their eyes when they'd faced off against eight armed men. She saw it there now. Pierre had sent the malware.

"Fuck." Pierre was out of his seat, tripping over his chair as he tried to get to her. "It's not what you think, Melinda."

She backed away. "It's exactly what I think." She forced the words out of her tight throat, her vision blurring with the sting of tears. "You sent the malware." She stabbed her finger at him. "You're the ones tracking my client. You *used* me."

"Melinda, no. Yes." Louis skirted the table, coming at her from the other direction, his hands held out in supplication. "Please, give us a chance to explain."

"Explain? You can't deny you sent the malware."

Pierre heaved out a sigh, straightening to his full height. "No, we can't. We did send it, and we are tracking your client, but Cordelia King is not who you think she is."

Melinda pressed her lips together, willing the tears away, but they refused to obey. MysticMage was Cordelia King? They knew her client's real name? Even she didn't know that. It could have only come from one person. Her client's husband. They'd said Wolf Enterprises was in security, but they also, it seemed, did private investigating. For wealthy people. Money could buy you a lot of support and a lot of skilled employees. It had bought them.

Louis took a few more steps toward her. "Cordelia King is an evil woman, Melinda. She's the one who's used you. Spun you a tale of a battered wife. It couldn't be further from the truth."

"She didn't spin me any tale. I recognized the signs."

"Did you? Or did you see what you wanted to see?"

"No, I—" Had she? Taken one look at the photo of a little old lady and jumped to conclusions? And what if she had? It made no difference. They'd used their malware to track her, moved in down the hall from her. Her instincts had been right. They *had* been stalking her.

Melinda shook her head. She didn't want to believe it. Not after what they'd shared over the last four days. The nights spent together, wrapping her in their warmth until morning. Louis ordering her favorite comfort food. Pierre thinking to grab her mother's teapot. Had it all been a lie?

"Why?"

"Cordelia King is a witch. An old, evil, time-traveling witch. She's targeted the Langeais wolves for centuries." Pierre held her gaze. "Last Christmas she tried to kill Gabriel and had Annabelle kidnapped. Then she disappeared. We've been trying to track her down for months. You were our best lead."

Melinda sucked in a breath. God, she'd been such a fool. Played right into their hands. They'd... She couldn't be here anymore. Couldn't look them in the face and not remember their intimate moments. Not after this. She snatched up her laptop. Manchu. She needed to get Manchu. And her purse, her phone, her passport. She headed for the stairs.

"Melinda, wait," called Louis. "Please. We're sorry. It was never our intention to hurt you. It's just when we met you..."

Pierre stood shoulder to shoulder with his twin, a united front. "It'll never happen again. We promise."

Melinda froze, one foot on the stairs. Those words. She'd heard them countless times before. Her father had said them to her mother every time he'd beaten her. All lies. He hadn't been sorry. It *had* happened again. And again and again.

Louis and Pierre crowded her in. Her gaze strayed past them to the door. She was their only link to Cordelia. Would they let her leave? She stared up the stairs where Manchu was probably curled up on the bed, oblivious to the drama unfolding. She loved the little guy. He was everything to her, but... She'd risk everything, including her client, if she didn't get out of here. She couldn't do it. She had to leave. Now. *Sorry Manchu. I'll come back for you if I can.*

Her heart breaking, she slipped past Louis and was across the living area before either of them had moved. She flung the door open and raced for the lift.

Stunned silence and then, "I'm going after her."

Louis. Footsteps followed her. Frantically, she pressed the lift buttons. The door swished open. Inside, she slammed down on the close door button, then the one for the lobby.

"Melinda," yelled Louis. "Wait, please."

"Let her go, Louis," commanded Pierre.

The door closed, and the lift was moving. She slumped against the wall and let the tears flow. *Let her go.* A sob bubbled up inside her. It had all been a lie. Everything. All along it had been them cracking the identities she'd set up for MysticMage. *She* was the job they'd had in London. And she'd fallen for it, for their charm. And for a minute there she'd thought they might tell her she was their mate.

Foolish, foolish Melinda.

The lift stopped and the doors opened on a busy lobby. She wiped away her tears and forced herself to move. She didn't have time to wallow in her misery. Pierre and Louis could change their mind. She needed to be long gone before Louis convinced Pierre they still needed her. Her passport was in the safe and she had no visa. No purse and no phone. But she did have her laptop. With that she could achieve a lot.

She'd hole up in some random hotel. It would take her a few days, maybe a week, to get things sorted. Not enough time for Pierre and Louis to track her through their malware again. If they could at all. Her virus would have done a number on Pierre's laptop.

There were numerous hotels on this strip — one of them would suffice. One night, just to organize everything online, then she'd disappear for good.

And Manchu?

Fresh pain bloomed in her chest, and her steps faltered. Maybe she could find a way to sneak back in a few days' time and steal him away. After everything Annabelle and Stef had told her about shifters, she doubted it.

She pushed through the entrance, blinking back tears. *I'm sorry, Manchu.*

"Well, look what we have here." Two men blocked her way. Two men with tattoos peeking out from under their collars. "Going somewhere, little hacker?"

* * * *

Louis slammed the door and stormed back into the suite. She was gone. Their mate was gone. He picked up a chair and threw it at the wall before rounding on his brother.

"Fuck you, Pierre. We should have told her!" Louis jabbed himself in the chest. "I *wanted* to tell her, but no, *you*" — he stabbed his finger at his brother, the pain of Melinda leaving fueling his fury — "*you* decided we shouldn't."

"You think it would have ended any differently had we told her?" Pierre shot back. "We betrayed her, Louis. Lied to her. *Putain*, we stalked her. Bought an apartment in her building, hacked into her security feeds and watched her make tea."

Louis prowled back and forth in front of his brother. He itched to throw another chair at the wall. Better yet, turn wolf and shred the fucking sofa, the entire suite.

Anything to appease the agony threatening to swallow him whole. "So, what, we just let her walk away? Why didn't you let me go after her?"

"She'll be back."

Louis gaped at his brother. "Why *the fuck* would she come back?"

"Think, Louis. Where is she going to go? She can't return to London. She doesn't have a valid visa to be here."

"Melinda's a hacker, *tête de noeud*, and she has her laptop."

"And we have Manchu."

Louis paused and glanced up the stairs. Melinda loved that ball of fur, but did she love it enough to risk coming back for him? After what they'd done?

"Give her some space, Louis. Let her think about things. She won't go far. Probably to the café downstairs. This place is crawling with shifters. And warded. She won't leave without Manchu."

The landline rang, and Pierre snatched it up, his body tensing as he listened. He dropped the phone back in its cradle.

"What is it, Pierre?" From the look on his brother's face, it wasn't good news.

"That was the front desk. Melinda left the hotel with two men. It didn't appear as though she went willingly."

"I thought Gabriel said we could count on the shifters in this hotel?"

"We can. But there's a dentist's convention starting tomorrow. The lobby is full of people checking in. They couldn't get to her in time."

Pierre turned to his laptop, cursed and swiped the useless thing to the floor. "Get onto the security feed.

See if you can track them to a car. I'll call Gabriel for backup."

Louis was already typing, hacking into the Ritz-Carlton's security system. "I'm in."

There she was, rushing out of the elevator. He tracked her through the crowded lobby. When she disappeared from that feed, he switched to the one at the front entrance. There. Two men. He zoomed in. Above the collar of one man, the hint of a tattoo. *Putain.* He slumped over his keyboard, his hands in his hair. The Faucherians had their mate.

Louis leaned in again, following their progress to an SUV, the license plate blurry, but visible. He locked in on it. He could trace it through the city's CCTV. It wouldn't be hard. The SUV was red. It was like they weren't even trying... He sat back. Because they weren't. This was a trap. To spring it, they were going to need backup.

* * * *

"Fuck you, Gabriel." Pierre threw his phone at the wall. It cracked and made a satisfying dent in the plaster. His claws extended, he punched them through the sofa cushions. Once, twice, a few more times until he'd shredded one, the floor covered with its stuffing. For once, he could see the appeal of unleashing his temper.

"Pierre?" Louis stood, laptop in hand, staring at the destruction he'd wrought.

"Gabriel thinks this is the perfect time for them to send Isobella to the tenth century. He's gathering the coven. Stef is with him."

"But...Melinda? Our mate?"

Pierre's gut curdled. "She's to be the distraction."

"It's a trap, Pierre. We can't go in alone. What about the backup Maxime was sending?"

"Gabriel's taking most of them, too. He's sending us Elliot and Alois."

Four werewolves and no witches against Cordelia, and how many Faucherians? Did they stand a chance? Did Melinda? Their mate was human. Fragile. He hung his head. Louis was right. They should never have let her go.

"The Proulx brothers are good in a fight. So are we. And we have the smarts and tech on our side." Louis nodded. "*Oui*, I think it's possible, if we plan it right."

Since when had Louis ever planned anything?

"Gabriel's right, Pierre. This is the perfect opportunity to get Isobella back into the tenth century. We're running out of time. She has to go. For all of us."

Louis as the voice of reason? Oh, how their roles had reversed.

"She's our mate, Pierre. We can do this. What other choice do we have?"

Chapter Twenty-Seven

The car sped through the streets of San Francisco with Melinda squeezed in the back between two burly tattooed men. No chance to escape. They'd bundled her into a car and peeled away from the curb before could utter a word or scream for help, her laptop seized by the guy in the front passenger seat. He was trying to crack her password. If she weren't so terrified, she might have found his ham-fisted attempts amusing.

Melinda hugged her body tight. Who were these guys? And where were they taking her? She side-eyed the guy to her right, the top half of his elaborate F tattoo visible above his collar. The last time she'd faced one of these guys alone, he'd held a gun to her head, prepared to kill her. And in the warehouse...

Is that where they're taking me?

It'd be the perfect place. Deserted. Close to the water. Any number of things to weigh her body down with when they tossed her into the harbor. The twins weren't coming to save her this time. They didn't know they'd grabbed her outside the hotel. Even if they did, would they attempt a rescue from these…whoever the hell these guys were?

Faucherians. That's what Louis had said back in the suite. Is that what they called themselves? It fit with the tattoo. But… Her throat tightened. Pierre and Louis had sent the malware. They'd lied to her and betrayed her. They'd *used* her. Could she believe anything the twins said anymore?

I'm so in over my head. Werewolves. Witches. Armed men with neck tattoos. She couldn't trust any of them.

The hub of the city receded, the streets getting wider and office buildings becoming houses. Melinda tried to keep track of the turns, the landmarks, but she was soon lost. One thing she knew, this wasn't the way to the docks. They were taking her somewhere else. But where?

The car slowed and they turned down a street, the houses stately manors, the neighborhood quiet. It did little to settle her nerves. Mob bosses lived in mansions, in gated communities, didn't they?

They pulled into the driveway at the back of a three-story home, driving straight into the garage. The home of Robert King, her client's husband? Or this Regis Veilleux Pierre had spoken of? Or was she to be dragged in front of Maxime, the alpha of the Langeais wolves? No. The twin's betrayal twisted in her gut, but she didn't think they were working with these Faucherians. Louis had killed the guy in her flat. Pierre, Louis and Gabriel had torn six of them apart in the warehouse.

Cordelia had warned Melinda that her husband had money. He could have hired this Veilleux and his tattooed men. He could have hired Wolf Enterprises.

Or both. Put a bounty on his wife's head. Winner takes all. That was the only scenario that made any sense.

The garage door closing behind them made her jump. Strong arms pulled her out and, despite her struggling, pushed her toward a door. It opened on a lift. The house had its own damned *lift*? Money. It bought a lot of things. Was it about to buy her silence?

The air in the lift was suffocating, the walls pressing in as soon as the doors closed. Melinda wanted to vomit. She wanted to cower. She wanted the security of the Ritz-Carlton and the two sexy men who'd protected her so far.

The lift stopped and Melinda was a split second away from hyperventilating. The door slid open on a living area decorated in cream and gold, with antiques and fine art that put the penthouse suite in the Ritz-Carlton to shame. She sucked in fresh air, but it did nothing to ease the tightness in her chest, or the nausea threatening to overwhelm her. Was this it? Was her life to be snuffed out? Not here. Not on the cream carpet, surely?

Three people — a woman and two men — stood with their backs to her. There was a nervous-looking couple by the window. And… Her vision narrowed. On the brocade chair in the center of the room. On the woman sitting in it. Like a queen overseeing her subjects. MysticMage.

No. It…it couldn't be. It wasn't… But it was. MysticMage. Or rather, Cordelia King.

Gone was the frail old lady with the frightened, haunted look that reminded Melinda so much of her mother in her last few years. This woman would've given the Iron Lady pause. The steel in her smile, the cold, flat stare. An evil witch. A time-traveling witch.

That's what Pierre had called her. And she was in *no way* a captive.

Oh God. They'd told her the truth. The twins. It all tumbled into place now. The email she'd sent to MysticMage, warning her, mentioning Pierre and Louis by name. The lack of a reply. The intruder breaking into her flat hours after she'd sent it, trashing her computers. There to kill her. How quickly Cordelia had agreed to meet, in an abandoned warehouse of all places.

She tried to kill Gabriel and kidnapped Annabelle.

They'd tried to tell her, but she hadn't listened. So convinced Cordelia was another poor soul who needed saving, so hurt by what they'd done, Melinda hadn't stopped to think. To listen. She'd fled. Not willing to hear another word from them.

Louis, with his love of food, who wore his heart on his sleeve. And Pierre—dominant, controlled, thoughtful. He'd rescued Manchu and her mother's teapot. For her. Sure, they'd lied to her. Betrayed her, but they'd also saved her. Twice. They'd each taken a bullet for her.

Louis and Pierre... They'd done the wrong thing by her, but they weren't the enemy.

"Our cipher is here. Excellent." The unusual blue and green gaze Melinda had become so familiar with over the last three months raked over her. "I'll deal with you in a moment."

Cordelia turned back to the young woman in front of her. "You have your orders, Grace. See that you follow through." That terrible smile again, as she held a wrinkled hand out to encompass a couple standing by the window. "Your mother's position in this family depends on it. You may go."

The woman nodded and made a beeline for her mother, embracing her as though it might be the last time she'd have the chance. Maybe it was. Grace glanced at Melinda as she left the room, a well of sympathy in her dark eyes. If Cordelia could threaten a member of her own family, what would she do to Melinda?

"Bring her forward."

A voice as icy as the River Thames in winter sliced through her misery. Rough hands dragged her forward. What she wouldn't give to have the twins by her side right now.

"You've caused me a lot of trouble, girl." A disapproving frown added lines to Cordelia's face. "A tiny slip of a thing, aren't you? What they see in you, I'll never understand." Her gnarled hand clenched around the armrest. "The Langeais wolves have always made poor choices in women, but you are useful to me still. Veilleux." Cordelia beckoned forward one of the men in front of her. "Are you ready?"

So this was Veilluex. The leader of the Faucherians. A Hugo Boss suit with a mercenary army at his command.

"*Oui*. I 'ave men stationed throughout ze house, on every floor and at every entrance. More men in ze gardens. If ze twins come, we will get zem."

Cordelia chortled, an unpleasant sound. "Oh, they'll come. Langeais wolves wouldn't shift in front of human. Not unless she were something special to them."

This was a trap? For the twins?

"She iz zeir mate?" Veilluex's predatory smile would have been at home on an alligator. "Zen she will be a useful test subject in ze laboratory."

Their mate? Was he right? A tiny bubble of warmth blossomed in her chest. But… *Wait. Test subject? What the hell?* No. *No.* Melinda was *not* going to be the subject of some weird-ass science experiment. And it didn't matter what the twins had done. She couldn't let that happen to them, either. But what choice did she have? Even if she were to break free of the hands that gripped her, she'd never make it past all the men Veilluex had stationed about the house.

Phones rang. Both Veilluex and another man, one without a tattoo, put their phones to their ears. Veilleux cursed in French.

"Dutton?" Cordelia asked of the other man.

"That was Douglas. Gabriel is mobilizing, but not to come here. They're using the spell. Sending Isobella back in time. Gabriel has called in backup. Half a dozen more Langeais wolves have shown up."

"Do you have enough men, Veilluex?"

"We'll make it work." He gestured to her captors. "Lock her in ze attic. No one goes in or out. Dutton, you're with me. If we stop zis Isobella going back in time, none of the Montagnes will pose a threat ever again."

Chapter Twenty-Eight

Melinda stood in the dusty attic, the door locked and two guards posted outside. They had her laptop and her purse. She had a few boxes and a tiny window too high for her to reach. She also had these.

Melinda unclenched her hand and stared at the lighter and the tiny red pouch of...something. Grace. The woman from earlier. The one who Cordelia had manipulated into to doing who knew what by threatening her family. She'd stumbled into Melinda on the stairs, shoving it into her hand. "Burn it," she'd whispered in her ear before apologizing to Melinda's captors and moving on as though she'd not a care for her predicament at all.

Getting out of the attic was one thing. Getting past all Veilluex's men was another. But it was a big house, and Melinda's childhood had been a master class in hiding. If she could get her laptop and find somewhere to hide, she might have a decent chance of escape. Of hacking into their security system. Better yet, hacking into their Wi-Fi and finding a way to contact Pierre and Louis. She had to warn them this was a trap. Warn them Veilleux and some guy named Dutton were on their way to stop Isobella from going back in time. And she had to tell them they were right, and she'd been wrong about Cordelia. So wrong.

She peered into the pouch. Herbs? Something witchy? A potion? She resisted the urge to sniff the leaves. Melinda eyed the gap beneath the door. She'd need something to cover her face, and something burnable to make a fire, but it was worth a try.

Melinda opened one of the boxes. *Old books. Perfect.* She chose a cookbook with glossy pages and lay it open on the floor, close to the door, but not against it. When the guards opened the door, they wouldn't knock her little fire over onto the timber floors. She wanted out of the attic, not to burn the whole house down with her in it.

From several brittle paperback crime novels, she tore pages and crumpled them up, placing them over the image of a crème brûlée. Probably another of Louis' favorites. She added more pages to her little pile. If she got out of this alive, she could ask him. She'd want to ask him, and Pierre, more important things than that. Like, were they ever going to tell her it was them who'd sent the malware? Had it all been a lie? Had she meant anything to them at all?

She squeezed her eyes shut. It still hurt. Their betrayal. Melinda could understand why they'd tracked her. To get to Cordelia. But everything else that had happened *after* they'd found her... How much of *that* was a lie? Making tea together. Their nights spent in the big bed, the way they'd worshiped her body as though she were the most precious thing in the world.

Cordelia and the Veilleux guy seemed to think she was their mate. From a logical standpoint, it made sense. Would they have divulged they were werewolves to her had she not been? That wasn't something you bandied about to just anyone. And Gabriel, telling her Pierre and Louis would have died for her that day in the warehouse? That *had* to mean something, right?

She'd never find out if she didn't get the hell out of here.

She crumpled more pages until she had a decent sized pyre, then wrapped her coat around her face, covering her mouth and nose, and lit the pile. As the fire took hold, she sprinkled the contents of Grace's little pouch onto the flames. With another cookbook, she fanned the smoke, pushing it under the door.

Melinda stepped back. The smoke now had a distinct smell, like...sage? Grace had given her *sage*? Was this some kind of joke? She was going to...what? Overpower two men with a cooking herb?

Her little fire flared as the attic door opened.

"*Putain.*" A tattooed man stared at her flames.

A second man pushed through the door, her open laptop in his hand.

Yes.

The cookbook was on fire now, and the room stank worse than a hippie gathering in the nineteen seventies. He helped his companion stomp it out, both of them breathing in lungfuls of smoke.

Melinda waited, holding her breath, her face covered. This had to work. She had to believe Grace wouldn't have risked handing her something as benign as a common garden herb.

It started with a smile that turned into a chuckle. Then both men were laughing, one holding up his hand, staring at it as though he'd never seen it before. He touched the wall, her fire forgotten. He said something in French, and his friend stared in wonder, before raising his hand to the wall, too. Were they...tripping? She edged closer. Neither of them paid her any attention. She grasped the edge of her laptop, and he let her take it, too absorbed with what was happening with the wall. Nothing, as far as Melinda was concerned.

One of them turned, his glazed eyes looking right at her. She froze. He dropped to his haunches and with child-like abandon, he hopped about the room like a...like a *frog*. The one who had held her laptop giggled, then licked the dusty wall like it was a lollipop.

Thank you, Grace.

Skirting the smoke, tightening her coat around her face, Melinda backed out of the door, closed it behind her and locked the men in, their laughter the only sounds from within.

Now all she needed was a place to hide. Somewhere quiet where she'd remain undiscovered long enough to get a message out. Somehow.

* * * *

Through the windscreen, Pierre stared at the large manor house down the street. If he'd had any doubts they had the right place, Veilluex and a half-dozen men leaving in a black Escalade confirmed it. He'd checked their files on known Faucherians. All but one matched. It hadn't taken Louis long to identify him as Dutton

King. He'd had an idea where they were headed and he'd shot off a text to Gabriel. A single word. *Incoming.*

Beside him, Louis checked the security feeds of the surrounding houses while Alois and Elliot, their only backup, scouted the neighborhood. That it was a trap was a given. It wouldn't stop them going in after their mate, but they needed to be smart about it. They wanted to save her, not get her killed. She was so fragile, too human. As soon as they had her safe, that was going to fucking change. No more skirting around the subject. They were telling her everything, then they were going to make her theirs.

Pierre hated to admit it, but Louis had been right. Rather than preventing this scenario, keeping things from Melinda had led to it. If Melinda's life wasn't in danger, he and Louis might well have traded punches. For real. They hadn't done that beyond the training mats since they were young pups. "Anything on the feeds?"

"*Oui.* I count two men in the front garden behind the hedge, and two at the back." Louis swiveled his laptop, showing him the two in the front. "If they're armed, they're being discreet about it. Don't want the neighbors calling nine-one-one. No telling how many are inside."

"Less the seven who left earlier. They've had to split their forces, too."

"I guess Gabriel does know what he's doing, after all."

Pierre grunted. Maxime trusted Gabriel's judgment. They should, too, but it still irked him his brother was using their mate like a chess piece, another pawn in the war between them and the Faucherians. "And if Cordelia's here?"

Louis shook his head. "Not our primary objective."

No, but if he had the chance to take her out… It'd taken them months to find the witch. If they lost her this time, they might never get this close to her again. With any luck, she'd die of old age.

Louis grabbed his arm. "Pierre, look."

The image on the screen zoomed in on the house, but Louis wasn't touching the keyboard.

Louis gripped his arm harder, grinning. "It's Melinda. It has to be. Clever little cipher."

He didn't know if his heart would burst with pride or relief. The picture zeroed in on a window on the second floor.

Pierre pointed at the screen. "Look. On the window. Behind the curtains. What is that? Lipstick?"

Louis took control of the image and zoomed in close. "It's a message. A single word. *Trap.* Where the hell did she get a lipstick from?"

"Does it matter?"

A slender hand snaked up above the windowsill and wrote out another message. *Run. Oui,* it was a trap, but there was not a chance in hell they were running. They'd come for their mate. They weren't leaving without her.

* * * *

Pierre and Louis were here. She'd got all choked up when she'd hacked into the security cam on the house across the street and spied them sitting in the car. They'd come? Once again putting their lives on the line for her? But… Were they here for her, as Cordelia had suggested? Or were they here for Cordelia? Perhaps it was best if she wasn't here to find out. They'd hurt her enough already, and unlike her mother, she wasn't going to stick around to let them break their promise all over again.

Melinda discarded the lipstick she'd found in the bedroom's en suite bathroom. She'd warned them that it was a trap. If they chose to come after Cordelia, that was on them. She wanted no part in it. What she needed was to get out of here, get Manchu and then disappear for good. Go somewhere where there were no werewolves and no witches, time traveling or otherwise. The Greek Isles were sounding more and more appealing.

The clump of boots outside the door stilled her fingers on her keyboard. It was only a matter of time before someone discovered she was no longer in the attic. Concealed behind an ornate bed head beneath a window, thick drapes on either side, she was well hidden, but her hiding place wouldn't stand up to a concerted search effort. The footsteps passed without entering the room. She breathed a quiet sigh of relief. With any luck, she could count on the twins being a distraction. Then she'd make a break for it. While they were busy here, maybe she could sneak back into the penthouse and grab Manchu. And her mother's teapot.

Melinda switched to another open tab — the house's alarm system. Not a closed-circuit system. A bad move on their part, but perfect for her. She couldn't turn into a werewolf or fire a gun, but she had her own way of making chaos. While it was all going to hell in a handbasket inside the house, no one should notice her sneaking out of the back door.

Her finger hovered over her enter key as she listened. All was quiet. She grinned. Not for long. She hit enter. The alarm blared, ear-splittingly loud. For a minute, nothing happened. Then doors slammed, boots pounded on the stairway and shouted commands competing with the *whoop-whoop* of the alarm echoed through the house. Melinda flicked to another tab and set off the sprinkler system. Someone had been safety conscious when they'd renovated this house. It worked in Melinda's favor. Water sprayed from the ceiling. Curses, in French and English, receded down the stairs.

Melinda switched to another tab and checked the black SUV down the street. It was empty. Pierre and Louis were coming in. Tucking her laptop under her coat, she peered out from behind the bedhead. *Time to move.*

Chapter Twenty-Nine

The Faucherian guard didn't see him coming and in seconds Pierre had dispatched him and taken his weapon. On the other side of the garden Louis, with his own newly acquired pistol, signaled his readiness. Time to storm the house. They took out two more guards in the foyer before meeting up with the Proulx brothers on the stairs.

The sudden silence as the alarm cut off was a relief. Now he could pinpoint where the rest of the Faucherians were. It wasn't hard. When would these people learn they were dealing with werewolves?

He took the stairs two at a time, leaving the Proulx brothers to secure the rooms downstairs. On the second-floor landing, he caught a scent. He dragged it into his nose. Female and age, and something else. Something fetid and malignant with the sour taint of bitterness and hatred and decay. *Cordelia.* He eyed the stairs. Melinda was up there, on the third floor. Their mate. They'd come here for her. But...

"No, Pierre," whispered Louis. "Not this time."

"This might be the only chance we get."

Louis' lips flattened into a thin line, but he didn't refute him. Louis knew he was right. If they lost Cordelia, they might never catch her, and she'd be free to wreak more havoc.

"Go find Melinda. Keep her safe. I'm going after the witch."

Louis nodded and bounded silently up the stairs. Pierre followed his nose down the hall.

He stepped into a room full of shadows even his keen eyesight couldn't penetrate. Witchcraft. The smell was strongest here. His wolf held at the ready, close to the surface, he inched his way forward.

A dry and dusty chuckle echoed about the room. "You're too late, wolf."

The voice crawled over his skin like a thousand ants, raising the hair on the back of his neck.

"Show yourself, witch."

The shadows shifted, thick and suffocating, swirling around his face, whispering across his skin, taunting his eyes with glimpses of cream and gold opulence, a brocade chair, but no Cordelia.

He eased a few steps further into the room, his senses peeled, ready to lunge the moment he could pinpoint her.

"You made a mistake coming here."

The disembodied voice sent shivers along his spine. His wolf had never backed down from anything, but this woman, this witch, set him on edge like no other threat before. Where was she?

"You kidnapped our mate. Nothing would stop us from coming after you." His voice was little more than a growl, his vocal cords shifting, coarse hairs bristling on the backs of his arms. His wolf wanted out, wanted to take over.

Another cackle. "Oh, I knew *that*, wolf. That's why I had Veilleux bring her here."

Then what was she talking about?

"You should've stayed with your twin. Coming after me is going to cost you." A light flared — a match — and for a brief instant the flame cut through the shadows, laying bare the old woman standing over a bowl of herbs, malevolent glee in her mismatched eyes. "Make your choice, wolf. Me or them."

A scream ripped through the house. "Louis! No!"
Melinda.

The old woman dropped the match into the bowl of herbs and began chanting, but Pierre didn't care. He was out the door, bounding up the stairs. His twin howled, and the pain of it sliced through him. The sound cut off, leaving only the harsh breathing of human males and the broken sobs of their mate.

* * * *

Louis groaned. His throat and wrists burned and his wolf was silent. *Silver.* They'd bound him in silver. The slight deadening of his senses as he'd stepped into the room had warned him there was wolfsbane present, but with his cuff turned over to protect him, and the image of Melinda on her knees, the barrel of a gun pressed against her temple, nothing short of a silver bullet to the head would've stopped him from taking that step.

Filthy *fucking* Faucherians. He'd sworn the man threatening her would count his remaining lifespan in seconds.

It had been his undoing. That, and the copious amounts of wolfsbane they had stored in the room. Far too much for the small amount of silver of his wrist cuff to counteract. The *connards* had used it to good effect, and Louis had lost control of his wolf. Now he lay here, naked but for a few scraps of clothing, shackled in silver. Louis chuffed. Pierre would maintain Louis never had control, and he wouldn't be far wrong, but he swore to the fates he'd learn some if they ever got out of this situation.

He shifted, hissing as the silver shackles around his wrists and neck blistered fresh skin. *Putain.* It burned, but the hollow emptiness in his mind, the absence of his wolf, hurt more. And hearing the sobs of their mate…

"*Chouquette.*"

Melinda lifted her tear-stained face. "I'm sorry," she mouthed.

He shook his head. "*Non, bébé.* I'm sorry. We're both sorry. We should never have deceived you." If not for their betrayal, she wouldn't be here. "It's going to be okay, Melinda."

˙ He grunted as a Faucherian kicked him in the ribs. "Quiet. Filthy animal."

Louis would have growled and chewed his ankle off if he could've called forth his wolf. "I'm going to rip out your throat the moment I'm free."

The *fils de pute* laughed. "Brave words, but zey mean nozing." He leaned in close. "I'm going to personally put a bullet in your 'ead ze moment you're no longer needed."

Another Faucherian walked into the room. "You could be waiting a while. Veilluex wants this one alive."

An American accent. The Faucherians' reach was spreading far and wide.

"And he's in a foul mood. Things didn't go so well with their lot."

Did that mean Isobella's trip back in time was successful? If he could have, Louis would have fist pumped the air.

"*Merde.* What does he want him for?"

The American shrugged. "Something to do with some organization. What was it called? The DGSE."

The Directorate-General for External Security? *Putain.* Pierre would have his balls if he ended up in the clutches of France's foreign intelligence agency. Not to mention Maxime. Louis wasn't keen about the idea of being a science experiment in a lab, either.

"What about ze others?"

"Veilluex wants the twin alive. The others..." The American shrugged. "If we can catch 'em, great. If not, kill 'em. I'm tired of these shifter fuckers stealin' our women. A little payback is in order."

Louis didn't need to wonder why they needed him and Pierre alive. Science had been using twins for their studies, their experiments for years.

"And ze *fille*?"

"You mean the girl? She goes with them. Some guy Veilleux calls the Doctor wants to witness a turning."

Fils de pute. Louis had to get out of these silver shackles. Had to warn his brother of the high concentration of wolfsbane in this room. He had to save their mate. For the first time in his life, he regretted his impulsiveness. Wished he was more like his twin. He prayed they weren't all destined to die in a science lab because of it.

* * * *

Pierre paused at the top of the stairs, straining to hear the muted voices down the hall. Why could he not make out their words? He sniffed the air. Nothing strong or tangible. He checked his wrist cuff. Still in place, the burn of the silver against his skin a constant. But there was wolfsbane here. There had to be. His senses were there, but not as strong as they should be. The Faucherians had increased the quantities. The silver against his skin was doing its job. His wolf wasn't coming forth uncalled for, but he wasn't unaffected.

With cautious steps, he made his way down the hall. The closer he got to the room, the greater the effect of the wolfsbane. They must have barrels of the stuff in there. His fear for his twin and his mate urged him to rush forward, but he contained it. He would be of no use to them if he, too, fell victim.

The soft rumble of his brother's voice filtered through the closed door. He was alive. *Thank the fates.* Louis grunted, then hissed. Melinda sobbed. They were both alive. *Thank fuck.* He would never forgive himself if his decision to go after Cordelia had resulted in their deaths.

Behind him, on the stairs, Alois and Elliot approached. He held up his hand, halting them, and pointed to his cuff. They nodded their understanding, poised, waiting. His phone vibrated in his pocket. He ignored it. If it was Gabriel, the fucker could wait. If this all ended badly, if he lost his twin and his mate, he'd beat his brother to a bloody pulp.

He eased next to the door, listening. It was a strain, with his senses muted, but he still far surpassed the abilities of any human. Louis and Melinda. And two men—one French, one American—discussing their plan to ambush him. One paced in front of the door. Pierre let his canines slide down.

Stupid *connard*.

He raised his weapon, waited until the *Americain* was clear of Louis and Melinda, then fired a short burst at head height through the door. He didn't miss. The body dropped to the floor with a thud. Shocked silence, and Pierre used his advantage and kicked the door open.

Fuck. No.

A fury he'd never experienced before roared through him at the sight that greeted him. Louis shackled in silver on the floor. Melinda, beside him, on her knees, the Frenchmen's hand twisted in her hair, holding a pistol to her temple, sobbing, pleading him with her eyes to help them.

No one put Melinda on her knees but them. Especially not some *connard* Faucherian.

"Do it," his countryman taunted him. "Shift. Only your wolf can save her."

Pierre smirked. His wolf would've liked nothing more than to rip this *fils de pute's* throat out, but the Faucherian was wrong. Shifting wasn't the only way to save her. And Pierre was too disciplined to be goaded into making that mistake. Not with all that wolfsbane. He wouldn't be stepping foot in the room, and he wouldn't be shifting. All he needed was a clear shot.

Louis lunged, knocking Melinda aside. Pierre fired. The Faucherian's head flew back, and he dropped, dead before he hit the ground. The Faucherian had made more than one mistake tonight. He and Louis were a team.

He leaned against the door frame. Both his twin and his mate were safe. For a minute, as he'd faced Cordelia, he'd thought he might have lost them both.

Louis crawled over to the dead *Americain* by the door, grabbing a set of keys from the man's pocket. "Nice shooting." He unlocked the shackles from around his wrists and neck and tossed them across the room. "That is an experience I don't want to repeat." The skin on his neck already beginning to heal, he scooped Melinda in his arms and pulled her into the hall, dark hair sprouting along his arms and bones cracking in his legs. "We need to stop doing this, *chouqette*. No more men pointing guns at you, *d'accord*?"

Pierre ushered them along the landing, away from the cursed wolfsbane, and Louis' wolf receded.

"I'm sorry." Melinda sniffled against Louis' chest. "I should've stayed hidden. I thought they'd be too busy dealing with you to notice me sneaking out. But he caught me. Then he caught you."

"Running away from us again, were you? Hm?"

"Cordelia was here. You didn't need me anymore."

Her words were muffled against Louis' shoulder, but it didn't mask the tremor in her voice. Pierre dropped his weapon and pressed his body against her back, wrapping his arm around her, so between them they encircled her. How could she think that?

Louis, his expression bleak, brushed his hand against her cheek. "Ah, my little *chouquette*. We were always going to come for you. Pierre... Pierre thought you might need some space. Some time to think alone. We figured... Manchu was upstairs. You wouldn't leave without him. Then we got a message from the front desk that someone had bundled you into a car outside the hotel. We came as fast as we could."

Pierre cupped her chin, forcing her to look at him. "We came for you, Melinda. Not Cordelia."

Melinda glanced between them, the vulnerability in her eyes nearly breaking him.

Louis rested his forehead against hers. "You're ours, Melinda."

"You're our mate," Pierre clarified, making sure there was no misunderstanding. A tear slid down her cheek, and he brushed it away. "I knew it the first day I met you in the lift."

"And I knew the moment you opened the door to me when I invited you to our apartment." Louis' smile was all cheek. "To taste my nuts."

She blinked at them. "You did? But what about...?"

"Cordelia?" Pierre heaved out a sigh. "We tracked you to get to her, but when we met you—"

"—we decided we were going to keep you." Louis set Melinda on her feet and cupped her face in his hands. "We wanted to tell you, but—"

"—we were afraid you wouldn't believe us about Cordelia." Pierre rested his chin on the top of Melinda's head. "I was afraid. Louis wanted to tell you sooner. We should've told you sooner."

Alois cleared his throat. "Maybe we should save the heartfelt conversations for later."

Both he and Louis growled at him.

Alois shrugged. "Suit yourself, but with the alarm going off and those shots fired, a neighbor is sure to have called the police. Given we're the only ones left standing—not counting the two tripping in the attic— we don't want to be here when they show up."

"And we need to warn your brother," piped up Melinda. "That Veillieux guy took a bunch of men to stop Isobella going back in time."

"We saw them leave." He gave her shoulder a squeeze. "I let Gabriel know.

"What about Cordelia?" asked Melinda.

Louis quirked an eyebrow at him.

"She escaped. I had a choice. Take out the old witch, or save my mate and my brother." He wrapped his arms around them both. "I chose the two of you. I will always choose you."

* * * *

In the back of the SUV, Pierre cradled Melinda in his lap. He had a need to claim her, here, now, in the back seat of the SUV. Urgency had his body thrumming with an impatience more familiar with his twin. He shared a look with Louis. He was feeling it, too.

Melinda squirmed, snuggling closer. The scent of her arousal filled the car as her fingers fiddled with his collar. All the blood in his brain headed south. "Drive faster."

Alois grinned, but he put his foot on the accelerator.

They pulled up in front of the Ritz-Carlton and he was out of the car before it had stopped moving. With Melinda tucked under their arms, he guided them through the foyer.

The elevator was full of people—of course it was—and they gave the trio strange looks. Melinda tucked between them, Louis in a pair of gray sweatpants and his chest bare. Pierre didn't care. They should be grateful he had enough control of himself not to fuck Melinda up against the elevator wall right in front of them. It was a close call, but he gritted his teeth and held on.

The elevator doors slid open on the penthouse floor, and Pierre propelled them through the vestibule to find Gabriel waiting for them. *Now* his brother deigned to show up. "Not now Gabriel."

Gabriel's nostrils flared, but he nodded. "We will talk later. Just know Isobella has gone back in time, but it wasn't without its problems. Her ex-fiancé, Douglas, grabbed hold of her at the last minute and went through with her."

Pierre skidded to a halt. It was difficult for his brain to process anything with his mate in need of claiming. "Will that change things?"

Gabriel shrugged. "We're all still here."

That was good enough for him.

"Stef's gone after them," said Gabriel.

Stef? How the hell had that happened? And who was going to tell Maxime his little sister had gone back in time?

"But that's a story for another day." He held a leather cuff with the silver wolf motif. "I take it you'll be needing this?" He tossed the cuff to Pierre. "I had every faith in you. In both of you." He settled his gaze on their mate. "Welcome to the Langeais wolves, Melinda."

"Thanks, brother." They'd have to tell him the Faucherians were upping the quantities of wolfsbane, reducing the effectiveness of their wrist cuffs. But not now. Not with their mate back in their arms. Pierre scowled at Gabriel. "Get the fuck out."

Gabriel chuckled, but complied. At the door, he turned. "Everything you need is in the master suite. I'll see you three in a week."

Pierre had them halfway up the stairs before the door had closed behind Gabriel. He wasn't waiting any longer. "Melinda, it's time to claim you as our mate."

Chapter Thirty

Melinda stared at the big bed. *We came for you, Melinda. Not Cordelia.* That's what Pierre had said. From Louis — *you're ours. Our mate.* Those simple words, their heartfelt admission, *Pierre's* admission he was afraid to tell her, had at once soothed her and ignited a pounding in her heart and her clit. What that would've cost her reserved lover to admit. And Louis, he'd barreled into that room without a thought for his own safety. To get to her. To save her. Again. Pierre, he'd had the chance to take down Cordelia. It's what they'd come here for. What his pack wanted. But he'd chosen her.

Now they were going to claim her. In this bed. Louis and Pierre. The thought of it made her knees weak.

Pierre opened the bedside drawer and set out a pack of medi-swabs and three syringes. *The turning is painful,* Pierre had told her, the taste of key lime pie lingering on her tongue as she stared at him over the glass coffee table. *It would last for three days. They would sedate her.*

Louis stepped in front of her, blocking her view. He cupped her cheek, and she leaned into his palm.

"You're overthinking this, *chérie*. Relax." He trailed his hand down, pausing over her heart. "Feel, not think."

Her heart thudded beneath his hand. He held it there for a moment, before shifting it lower until he was cupping her breast, rubbing his thumb across her nipple. He pressed his lips to hers—a gentle touch. As he trailed soft kisses over her cheek, Melinda found it hard to do anything *but* feel.

Louis paused at her earlobe. "Trust us," he whispered, then dipped to her throat.

Pierre joined them, his hand cupping her other breast. The scrape of his teeth as he nuzzled her jawline sent shivers down her spine. Should she be frightened? Should she be running for the hills?

Pierre dipped to her throat. "We'll take care of you, Melinda. Let us claim you."

The two of them, in tandem, nipped at her skin. Her whole body trembled. Their scent, their bodies, wrapped around her, their mouths on either side of her throat…it was the most erotic moment of her life. Yes, she wanted this. Wanted them. And as insane as it sounded, she wanted them to bite her. Both of them.

"Say it, Melinda. Give us permission."

There was a punch of command in Pierre's voice. He was asking for consent, but he wouldn't take no for an answer. It should be sounding alarm bells, but all her mind was producing was the fury on their faces when they'd set eyes on her, on her knees, a gun to her head. First Louis, then Pierre. Gabriel was right. They would *die* for her.

They waited for her reply, not pressuring her for a response.

"Yes."

Then they were gone, both of them and she stood, bewildered and bereft.

Louis chuckled. "Our mate is impatient, Pierre." He shucked his sweats in one smooth motion.

Pierre, a neat pile of clothes at his feet, stood proud beneath her gaze. Were it not for the expression in his eyes, the whirlpool of emotion, she'd have thought him unaffected. But this was Pierre. Calm on the surface, deep feelings underneath.

He cocked his head to the side, the hint of a smile playing across his lips. "Let's not keep her waiting."

Then he was moving, cupping her face and kissing her lips, plundering her mouth with his tongue. His hands made short work of her blouse and bra as Louis removed her jeans and panties. She was naked. They were naked. This was happening.

With a jerk of Pierre's chin, Louis lay down on the bed. Biceps bunched as he hooked his hands behind his head. Knee raised, the evidence of his arousal jutting against his stomach, he grinned at her like some nude centerfold. Such a tease. In his eyes, the promise of so much more.

He held out his hand to her, and with Pierre's palm on the small of her back urging her forward, she took it and let him help her onto the bed to straddle his lap. His hot, hard length trapped against her core, she rode his hips, sliding back and forward as he palmed her breasts. She was so close. Knowing Pierre watched, that he got off on watching, spurred her on.

Pierre settled in behind her, gripping her hips and holding her still. "*Non, non.* Not without me. Not this time." With a tug on her calves, he resettled her flat against Louis' chest. "Together."

Pierre spread her wide, her thighs straddling Louis', baring her for his touch. He teased her slippery folds with two fingers before sliding them inside her. He knew exactly what she needed, how she needed it. Louis captured her moan with his mouth, and as though by silent communication, they set up a rhythm — Louis' tongue, Pierre's fingers, and the press of Louis' cock against her clit. As masterful as their malware code, they set off every trigger in her body. Played her like virtuosos — strumming her to a crescendo she might never come down from.

She broke, gasping for air, spasm after spasm, spurred on by the deep, satisfied rumbles of two males, one in front and one behind. With residual spikes of pleasure shooting through her, she dropped her head against Louis' shoulder.

Pierre curled himself over her, his weight on his forearms, caging but not crushing her. "Are you ready, *bébé*?"

Ready? No. Yes. Maybe.

"Should we both have her, Pierre? Claim her in all ways she can be claimed?"

Melinda stilled. All ways she could be...? She met Louis' eyes and saw the hope in them. Pierre ran his hands down the cleft of her ass. She couldn't help the flinch.

Pierre shifted his hand to her hip. "I don't think she's ready for that yet."

Louis pulled her mouth down to his and kissed her fears away. "Nothing you don't want, *chouqette*. Not until you're ready."

The head of Pierre's cock nudged her entrance. "So we're clear, Melinda. We're keeping you. Forever. We're going to protect you and love you for the rest of your life."

"*Non*," murmured Louis. "For the rest of *our* lives."

If ever there was a declaration, there it was. And she wanted what they were offering with every fiber of her being.

"Yes. I'm ready." To make sure they understood exactly what she was telling them, she said, "Bite me."

Pierre thrust inside her, filling her, and Louis rolled his hips. The friction was intense, the sensation overwhelming and as they worked together to bring her undone again, she gave herself over to it, dropped her internal walls and opened herself to them. Trusting them. Letting herself get lost in the pleasure storming through her body.

She barely noticed when they nuzzled her neck, one on either side. The rasp of their tongues over the pulse in her throat only added to the sensation between her thighs. The sting of teeth nipping at her skin sparked an insistent pressure at the base of her spine. She was close. Oh, so close.

Pierre thrust harder, hitting nerves deep inside her, and as her orgasm roared through her, they struck, latching onto her throat as they pounded her to heights she'd never experienced before. She screamed, but not from pain, her whole body convulsing between them as wave after wave of pleasure washed over her.

Louis licked their mate's throat, lapping at her wounds as Melinda collapsed on his chest. Before the turning could take hold, Pierre grabbed a syringe, prepped her limp arm, and gave her the sedative.

Melinda mumbled something as she snuggled into him, and it wasn't long before she was sleeping soundly.

For three days, they would keep her sedated, then her training would begin. Louis grinned. Training, he'd heard, was fun. Maintaining form was a skill all werewolves needed to learn. Mishaps occurred. Uncalled for shifts resulting in ripped clothes and naked bodies. His grin widened. When training one's mate, that meant lots and lots of sex.

Pierre growled at him. "I know what you're thinking, Louis."

He quirked an eyebrow at his twin. "And you're not?"

A smile tugged at the corner of Pierre's lips. *Oui*, his brother was looking forward to training their mate, too.

Pierre disappeared into the bathroom, returning with a wet cloth. As Louis cradled Melinda in his arms, Pierre cleaned her up. The twin puncture marks on either side of her throat, he left alone. Those would be the first things to heal as her body transitioned from human to werewolf.

With a toss of the cloth toward the en suite, Pierre joined them on the bed, and they cradled her between them.

Pierre brushed a strand of dark hair off her face. "She's ours now, Louis."

"Ours." And no stinking Faucherian was ever getting near their little mate ever again. Not while he still breathed.

Chapter Thirty-One

Two weeks later

Pain rippled through her as Cordelia forced her eyes open to a familiar scuffed timber floor, a cold fireplace and a simple slab table. She was in the one place she never permitted anyone to see. The one nobody except her knew existed, almost as humble as the little mud hut she'd grown up in. Unable, even after all the years, the centuries that'd passed, to turn her back on the memories of her roots.

She groaned, struggling to her feet, every bone, every muscle in her body on fire. She grabbed one of the many canes she kept around the place. Her body was too old and weak for her to use her time-traveling spell, but Veilluex had left her little choice.

Cordelia cracked her cane against a chair leg. *Fool of a man.* They'd known from the warehouse the Langeais wolves had a way to counteract the effects of wolfsbane, but Veilluex had had confidence in the barrels of wolfsbane he'd had shipped in, and his men. And, he'd argued, they had the woman, the cipher. And her. What werewolf could defeat the powerful Cordelia?

Except Cordelia was no longer as powerful as she'd once been. Her memory was fading as fast as her body, and without her grimoire, she had few spells at her disposal. Along with her home, it was something she'd allow no one to know about. Not even her kin. Her power to control them maintained only through their fear of what she could do to them. What she used to be able to do. She'd once boiled a man alive from the inside out. If only she could do that now.

Through the window, the afternoon sun dipped low. So she'd gone forward in time, but how far forward? She turned on the television and flicked through the channels until she found a news station. Two weeks. She'd gone forward two weeks.

Cordelia shuffled about the room, searching every nook and cranny. She checked all her secret hiding places. Every last one. Desperation fueled her search, her rage. Nothing. It wasn't there. Her grimoire wasn't there. It wasn't *anywhere*.

Her memories of that day taunted her. The tenth-century mud brick hut, rough and unkempt. Her drunken, useless son sprawled on the cot snoring. And Isobella Rodriguez flanked by two men—the brutish Montagne twins— storming in, tearing the place apart and taking her grimoire.

No. Cordelia slammed her cane down on the kitchen counter, splitting her stick in half.

Veilleux had *failed*. Isobella had gone back in time. Her grimoire remained lost. She wanted to scream, to rail against fate. Once again, she'd been unable to subvert that capricious bitch, fate.

She slumped into a chair, heaving. Grace. She still had Grace.

* * * *

"Well, if all it takes is for a book to distract you, I'm leaving."

Alain barely glanced at the stunning brunette glaring at him from across the room. The door slamming told him she'd left, but he didn't care. He couldn't tear himself away from the item that had arrived by special delivery. This was no ordinary book.

His trepidation grew with each blood-stained page he turned. Had he not been wearing gloves, he wasn't sure he'd want to touch the thing. An ancient grimoire with some of the vilest spells he'd ever encountered. This was the witch they were up against. And yet, from what Pierre had told him, she'd had ample chance to use a spell on them and hadn't. Was her power waning?

Some of these spells required hours of preparation — strength of mind *and* body. If Cordelia King was weakening, now was the time to strike. If they could find her again.

* * * *

Maxime downed the last of his cognac and pegged the empty glass at the wall. What was the point of drinking if he couldn't get drunk? If, no matter how much he drank, it did little to numb the pain. He'd gained one sister, only to lose another. Stefanie. Gone to him forever. He cursed the day his father had handed him his ancestor's journal.

He was a dominant *fils de pute* and he was never going to be anything but an alpha, but that came with responsibilities. Not all of them pleasant. Preparing Stefanie for what she would face had been one of the hardest things he'd ever done. Second only to giving her the amulet to ensure her fate.

Maxime glared at the journal on his desk. Everything outlined — their origins, Cordelia. Details of the women who were to go back in time and change the fate of the Langeais wolves. Erin Richardson, Rebekah Clarke, Isobella Rodriguez and... Maxime leaned on his desk. Stefanie d'Louncrais. His sister. Of all the things he'd read in the damn book, this cut him the deepest.

Beneath his ancestor's concise hand, a few lines in his sister's familiar scrawl. What she'd written, centuries ago, was the only reason he'd followed through with what needed to be done.

* * * *

Stefanie turned the golden amulet over in her hand. A sacred relic of the pack, imbued with magic centuries ago, and designed to protect and keep the Langeais wolves safe. Erin Richardson had found one and accidentally activated its spell and ended up in the tenth century, mated to Stef's ancestor. Rebekah Clarke had had a similar experience.

Maxime had given it to her last Christmas. An odd gift, with a cryptic message. She hadn't known what to make of it. Until Isobella had cast her spell to go back in time and that *connard*, Douglas, had followed her through. In that moment, she'd known what she had to do.

Coals glowed in the brazier in the corner, giving the room a soft glow. Lining the walls, chests overflowing with tomes and scrolls. The vaunted library of the d'Louncrais. The tenth-century version. On the desk before her, the one book that mattered.

A journal. One she'd seen many a time — her brother, Maxime, had pored over its pages for hours. It belonged to her ancestor, Gaharet d'Louncrais. *He* was in the great hall, surrounded by the heroes of her childhood tales — Ulrik Voclain, Aimon Proulx, Edmond and Aubert Montagne.

She picked up a quill and opened the book. One last letter to her brother, though he wouldn't read it for another eleven centuries. Stefanie dipped the quill into the ink and started writing.

* * * *

Grace handed her ticket to the flight attendant and boarded the plane, finding her seat in cattle class. With the magnitude of her mission, Cordelia could've at least stumped for a business class ticket. *Not that miserable old witch.*

She stared out of the window at the tarmac. Any other time, she'd be delighted to be flying to Paris. She'd always wanted to visit the city of love — climb the Eiffel Tower, walk along the Seine, visit the Louvre, gorge herself on French pastries. Would Cordelia forever ruin her thoughts of Paris?

Grace leaned against the headrest and closed her eyes. *Seduce Alain d'Louncrais. Get the grimoire. Save my mother.* If ever there was a person less suited to this task, it was her, but Cordelia had her over a barrel. She would do what she had to do. Including some old dude on the witches' council.

Epilogue

It had been one week and four days since Melinda had awoken a werewolf. Eleven days of not knowing her own strength, not being able to control her form and tearing through almost all of her clothing, Manchu not knowing what to make of her, and lots and lots of hot sex with her attentive mates.

Today, they'd given her a reprieve. She needed more clothes. Louis had suggested she not bother with clothes at all. That would have pleased him no end, her walking around perpetually naked. Pierre had sent for Annabelle. They'd never get *any* training done if she never wore any clothes. That hadn't seemed like a bad thing to Louis.

So here they were, Melinda swamped in one of Louis' T-shirts, crowded around the kitchen bench as Louis helped her prepare Kung Pao chicken. It wouldn't be so bad—she would have enjoyed chatting with Annabelle again, asking her a few questions about her turning as her mates talked with Gabriel — if Louis hadn't found her remote-controlled vibrator.

Pierre must have packed it when they'd left London. Whether he'd intended it to be used quite this way, Melinda would never know, but Louis had a devious mind. Why had she agreed to letting him insert it? Because he'd given her the choice of trying what he'd suggested on the night of her claiming — something she wasn't sure if she was ready for yet — or this.

She clenched her hand around the wok handle as Louis stuffed his hand in his pocket and hit the remote. Melinda shot him a glare, then focused on stirring the onions. Her whole body was primed. Louis knew what he was doing with that thing. Pressing that button at regular intervals, enough to keep her on edge, but not enough to send her over. Not yet, anyway.

But he would. Send her over the edge. A few more strategic presses of that button and she'd orgasm right in front of everyone. He'd get a kick out of that. As if they didn't already know what was going on. Annabelle winked at her. Yeah, they knew. Gabriel was too polite to say anything, though he sent a heated gaze in Annabelle's direction. Pierre… He was enjoying it in his own way.

Louis smirked. She did her best to ignore him, focusing on what Gabriel was saying with the attentiveness of a gamer about to lose her highest score.

"It's been two weeks since Isobella went back in time." Gabriel's hand dipped from Annabelle's hip to her ass, and he pulled his mate in closer. "We're still here. That's got to count for something."

Annabelle leaned into her mate. "I know she had to go, but I worry about her, how she's coping, how long it took before your ancestors found her."

Gabriel's grip on his mate tightened. "I know, *bébé*. I know you miss her, but this way she gets to live a long and happy life. Had she stayed…"

Pierre side-eyed her, before leaning his elbows on the countertop. "What about Stef? And how did Maxime take it when you told him?"

"I'm surprised he's not here." Louis pressed the button on the remote again. "Beating you to a pulp. He's always been over-protective of her."

Pierre's nostrils flared. Melinda elbowed Louis, glaring at him. He ignored her.

"He wasn't surprised when I rang." Gabriel snorted. "*Fils de pute* knew it was going to happen. He's the one that gave her one of the pack's amulets so she could do it."

Pierre straightened. "He *gave* her an amulet? Knowing she would use it to go back in time? How the hell did he know?"

Gabriel scowled. "That blasted journal he's got. The one written by Gaharet d'Louncrais and passed down to every alpha through the centuries, is far more detailed than he lets on. I'd love to get a good look at it, but Maxime keeps it hidden."

Louis pressed the damn button on the remote again, making her jump. Melinda kicked him in the calf. Louis sniggered. Pierre's attention snapped to her. Gabriel rolled his eyes. Another press of the remote and Melinda clamped down on a moan, her body twitching. She was so damn close.

Pierre's eyes narrowed on Louis. "Louis."

Louis pressed the remote again, holding it down for longer. "Mm?"

Melinda parted her mouth on a gasp.

Pierre held his hand out to Louis. "Give it over."

Oh, thank God. Thank you, Pierre.

Louis produced the remote and slid it across the counter. Annabelle and Gabriel followed its progress.

Melinda's already hot cheeks caught fire. She made a grab for it, but Pierre was faster, snatching it out of her reach.

Turn it off, Pierre. Please.

Pierre studied the little gadget for a minute, then a slow smile spread across his lips.

Oh, no.

He pressed the button. Once, twice, three times. Then held it on for a long minute. Melinda couldn't help the low moan that slipped out between her lips.

Annabelle grabbed her purse. "On that note, we're out of here. I'll get you some clothes and have them sent up to you. In a few hours. I think you guys are going to be busy for a while." She eyed her mate. "And so will we."

Gabriel rumbled his agreement.

At the doorway, Annabelle turned. "Have fun, sweetie."

Then they were gone, leaving Melinda with her two devious mates and that damn remote. She lunged for it, but Pierre held it above her head. He leaned over and switched off the gas on the cooktop. "I don't think we'll be needing food for a while."

Melinda bolted from the kitchen.

Louis chuckled behind her. "You can't run far enough away, Melinda. We have the remote."

As she reached the top of the stairs, Pierre pressed the remote and held it on. Melinda slid down the wall. *Yes.* She was going to… Pierre took his finger off the button and her orgasm slipped away. *Nooo!*

Louis started up the stairs, Pierre close behind him. "This is going to be fun."

Pierre scooped her up and carried her into the bedroom and tossed her on the bed. "*Oui,* I wish I'd remembered this sooner."

"I still think we should keep her naked for the next three months." Louis stripped his shirt away from her body. "Are you ready, *chouquette*?"

Melinda was more than ready.

Sign up for our newsletter and find out about all our romance book releases, eBook sales and promotions, sneak peeks and FREE romance books!

Want to see more from this author? Here's a taster for you to enjoy!

The Descendants: The Wolf and His Grace
K.E. Turner

Coming 2026

Excerpt

Backlit by the soft glow of the street lamps, the Gothic spires of the Musee de Cluny rose behind the modern façade of its reception building as Grace Williams stepped out of the cab.

What in the sweet tarnation am I doing here?

Her designer clutch tight in her white-knuckled grip and the Swarovski crystals on her dress shimmering with her every step, Grace presented her embossed invitation to the door attendant and entered the brightly lit foyer. She kept waiting for someone to stop her, to call her out as a fraud in a fancy dress, but no one did.

Directed to the stairs, her heels clicking on the tiles and her mouth drier than a cotton crop in the summertime, she crossed the floor mindful of every step. If she wasn't careful, she'd roll her ankle. Or worse, fall in a heap of yellow satin and heels. What she wouldn't give for her trusty flats or her sneakers, but they wouldn't fit in here any more than she did.

She'd only been this nervous once before in her life. Three days ago. And she'd had as good a reason then as she did now. The only thing worse than being summoned by Cordelia King, matriarch of the King family and rival for the role of the most evil old witch ever, was to be given a task by said witch.

Good golly gravy. Grace would give anything to be ensconced in the familiar smells and cozy clutter of Thrifty Witch, sitting behind her counter with a cup of herbal tea, doing a stock report, balancing the books even. She did not belong here. In Paris. At a charity event with a two-and-a-half-thousand-dollar ticket price. In this dress. Could not comprehend why Cordelia had deemed *her* suitable for *this* mission.

A glamorous couple overtook her on the steps in a splash of red satin and sequins and an expensive suit. Why hadn't Cordelia sent her great nephew, Dutton? She snorted, and the couple gave her the side eye. She fixed a painted smile on her face, and they continued on.

Grace knew why Dutton hadn't come, and that only made the butterflies in her stomach flap with the frenzy of a hurricane's wind. Alain d'Louncrais was a notorious playboy, so Cordelia had told her. With a preference for women. Then why not Irena King? The rumor doing the rounds of the coven had Irena stealing another witch's fiancé. Who better than someone with the moral compass of a hyena to undertake this mission? At least Irena had experience in seducing a man to get what she wanted.

Grace tripped on her dress, and would have face planted on the top step if not for the strong hand that gripped her elbow.

"Mademoiselle?"

She turned, smiling up at her savior, and her heart stalled. He had the most unusual eyes. One blue and one green. In a face that would haunt her dreams from here until eternity. Good dreams. Sexy, don't-tell-your-grandma-what-we-did kind of dreams.

Grace was staring and gaping like a guppy fish. She scrounged up some dignity. "Thank you, Monsieur. I…I mean, merci, monsieur."

He straightened, though he still had hold of her elbow, and the warmth of his hand was doing funny things to her insides. As was the sheer visual overload of gorgeousness standing before her. This is what they meant when they said a man filled out a suit to perfection.

"American, no?"

"Yes. I…I mean, oui. I'm visiting from le Americain. From California. It's my first time in Paris. I flew in yesterday morning for this event. Pardon, monsieur, I don't speak a lot of Francais." She'd heard the French liked it when you tried to speak their language, but a few days of Duolingo and a French phrasebook did not make her fluent. And she was babbling.

She must be doing something right, for he smiled at her, and oh, what a smile it was. Perfect teeth, dimples. She basked in it, her humble heart fluttering in its warmth.

"Well, mademoiselle, I hope you enjoy your time in Paris."

Then he released her elbow and continued up the steps, leaving her staring after him. She brushed off the pang of disappointment. Fancy dress aside, she was but a regular, average-Joe American girl who, through no choice of her own, found herself at this glittery event. On any other day, he wouldn't give her a second glance. Ordinarily, she'd never cross paths with a man like that. Him? Walking into her little store? In a Hallmark romance, maybe.

Wait. One blue eye, one green. Like Cordelia. Coincidence? Maybe. Or Cordelia had sent someone to spy on her. Make sure she got the job done. But Grace had met all the Kings. She would have remembered *that* guy.

The doorman looked expectantly in her direction, and Grace put her concerns about the dark-haired Frenchman out of her mind. She was here for one reason only. Find Alain d'Louncrais and steal an ancient grimoire from him. She stepped into the function room.

The thrum of voices, the clack of heels and the clink of wine glasses echoed across the vast space as ladies in evening gowns and men in suits mingled, nibbled on appetizers and chatted about whatever people discussed at fundraisers like these. Grace wouldn't know. She'd never been to one.

She accepted a glass of champagne from a circling waiter. Grace had no intention of drinking, but it would look odd if she didn't have a glass in her hand. Worse still if she asked for a glass of Coke, or apple juice. Events like these didn't cater for non drinkers. She pretended to take a sip, surveying the crowd of wealthy patrons of the Musee de Cluny. Which one of the dozen or so men in suits was Mr. d'Louncrais? What did a witch powerful enough to land a seat on the Council of Witches look like?

She'd Googled him and come up with zip. Not surprising. A witch wealthy enough to afford a shindig like this would have a team of techies scrubbing his existence from public record. He wouldn't be young. Cordelia King was the most powerful witch Grace knew, and that woman was ancient. One foot in a grave she couldn't fall into fast enough, as far as Grace was concerned. That would rule out half of the men here tonight.

She weaved her way through the crowd, offering smiles and pardons as she went. He was French, she knew that much. So that eliminated anyone without a French accent. Still too many to choose from. A waitress offered her a plate of mini cheesy pastries.

"*Excusez-moi, s'il vous plait*, I…I'm sorry, my French isn't that great." The waitress sniffed, but Grace plowed on. "Would you know which one of these gentlemen is Alain d'Louncrais? I'm meant to be meeting him here." Could she sound any more like a Tinder date? "My boss, he had to cancel at the last moment." Grace cringed as she made up a story on the fly. "Food poisoning. He sent me in his stead. Lucky me. I got a nice dress, expensive champagne, but I'm supposed to be meeting this Alain d'Louncrais here and I have no idea what he looks like." Grace smothered a cringe. Even to her ears, it sounded lame. *Fiddlesticks.* If she couldn't fool a waitress, how was she going to outsmart a witch smart enough to secure a position on the Council of Witches?

"Non, I do not." The French had definitely perfected the art of looking down their noses at someone. This waitress excelled at it. She held her tray out to Grace. "Gougeres?"

Grace waved her off. "Non. Merci."

Merci for nothing. The waitress moved away. Darn this stupid mission. And darn Cordelia. What was so important about this grimoire, anyway? Grace eyed the door. What was she doing here? She had little to no chance of success despite all her precautions. Grace had never had the capacity nor the inclination to be good a liar. Alain d'Louncrais would see through her and her spells. He would know in an instant why she was here.

As for stealing this grimoire… Witches protected their grimoires like a dragon would protect its hoard. An ancient grimoire coveted by other witches? It wouldn't be lying around for her to take. D'Louncrais would have it locked up and warded to the eyeballs.

The memory of her mother's pleading eyes held her in her place. She took another pretend sip of her champagne. Why, oh why had her mother had to go and fall for a member of the King family? If she hadn't, she'd have still been safe back in Alabama. Lonely, but safe. And Grace wouldn't be standing here in a pair of heels high enough to give her a nosebleed and a dress that wouldn't have looked out of place at the Academy awards..

"I believe the man over there is Alain d'Louncrais."

Grace turned to the woman behind her, with coiffed gray hair and a pair of diamond earrings worth enough money to feed a small army, her champagne glass directing her across the room.

"The man with the goatee?"

A tinkle of a laugh. "Non. Non."

The gentleman with the goatee and hair more white than gray moved away to greet someone.

"Him."

She followed the woman's appreciative gaze to a tall man, broad shoulders filling out his suit and dark hair tied back into a sleek ponytail. As if he knew he was the object of speculation, the man turned, and Grace's heart stuttered.

Witches on a broomstick.

It was him. Her gallant savior on the steps. The man with the gorgeous smile and two different colored eyes.

Son of a chocolate biscuit.

About the Author

K.E Turner can't remember a time when she wasn't writing stories or reading books — as a teenager in class instead of doing math, in her lunch break at work, or at home when there's housework to be done. With a love of history, mystery, suspense, paranormal, and romance, she likes combining more than one element in her stories.

An award-winning author, she writes spicy paranormal romances and romantic suspense, with strong but good hearted heroes, smart, sassy heroines and an often unexpected villain or two, to shake things up.

Based in a small village by the beach on the east coast of Australia, she lives with her husband and two dogs. A hopeless romantic, she enjoys sunsets over the water, walks on the beach, candlelit dinners and a nice shiraz.

K.E. Turner loves to hear from readers. You can find her contact information, website details and author profile page at https://www.firstforromance.com

ENTWINED PUBLISHING